In Fields of Butterfly Flames
and othe stories

In Fields of Butterfly Flames and other stories

Steve Wade

Steve Wade

Bridge House

British Library Cataloguing in Publication Data
A Record of this Publication is available from the British Library

ISBN 978-1-907335-87-7

This edition published 2020 by Bridge House Publishing
Manchester, England

Contents

Introduction

The stories in this collection first appeared in anthologies and periodicals. Some of them have won prizes or have been placed in writing competitions.

Ostracised by betrayal, isolated through indifference, gutted with guilt, or suffering from loss, the characters in these twenty-two stories are fractured and broken, some irreparably. In their struggle for acceptance, and their desperate search for meaning, they deny the past: *That Man's Father, Forever Chasing Pigeons*; forego reality: *In Fields of Butterfly Flames, Once There Were Rabbits, A Mother's Love*. Some abandon responsibility: *On the Seventh Day, The Panicked Rat, Van Gogh's Ear*. Others are running from something or someone: *High Flyer*. Some flee their homes and their homelands: *Downing Out in New York, Adios España Adios*; while others return home, only to find themselves even more marginalized and estranged: *Of Men and Dogs, A Strange Man About the House*.

A Mother's Love

She pretends to be my daughter. "No, Mommy. Please, Mommy, don't," she says. "I'm sorry, Mommy. I love you." Her bright eyes pleading desperately to infect me with the blindness she has brought to others.

Only I can see behind those green eyes, eyes that draw men to her the way the blue sea sucks bodies into its drowning waters.

Because of her this family is in ruins. The first thing she did was take him from me. Helplessly, I watched it happening in this very house where I had raised her as my own. The ankle-socked girlie-laugh could no longer disguise the swelling flesh, the intentional hitching up of the checked mini-skirt, revealing sinful thighs, as she prostrated herself on the couch before the TV in the evenings.

My heart bled to see him peering out from behind his newspaper – a black panther sizing up its prey in a jungle clearing from behind a mesh of snarled vines. Except the doe-eyed antelope innocently grazing on popcorn was its own lure. Prey to entrap the predator.

I begged God to severe the umbilical cord attached to this gestating horror. I promised to be a better wife, to never again deny my husband the rightful pleasures bestowed upon him by our matrimonial union. No use. The pull of the drowning waters was, for my husband, too strong, the temptation to swim into the voluptuous horror too great.

Even then I did not despair. My faith was full. I persevered. I approached God on His terms. If He gave me back my husband and my child, I was willing to forgive, if unable to forget. The rest of my life I vowed to dedicate to Him, to the spreading of His Gospels. I was ready to endure discomfort and pain, to undergo hardship, to rise long before daybreak in deepest winter, to fall to my knees before His image and worship for hours, until my body gave way to fatigue and famine.

All in vain. That's when I knew that somehow I had spawned one of the Devil's minions, if not the Devil incarnate.

In the early stages, this thing confined its abominating ways to those occasions when I was absent. But I saw it in their smug and satiated faces on my return from morning worship. He, who never whistled, whistling as he pottered about the house, hands in pockets, his eyes, like a serpent's tongue, flicking at that thing, tasting the air between them. And she, it, stretching shamelessly on tiptoe to reach something in the high kitchen cupboard, already goading him, tempting him with her indecent white flesh for the next encounter.

Soon even the thin veil of supposed normality was cast aside. Responding to her demonic summons, he was compelled to leave our marriage bed deep in the night-time. With my hands clamped against my ears, I'd pray aloud to deaden her hedonistic screams woven into his heavy grunts. I prayed that He might at least spare me the sickening sounds of betrayal by removing my sense of hearing. But it was He who chose not to listen.

Forsaken. I had been forsaken. But wait. Was not this a test of faith? After all, had He not put his own son through just as great an ordeal? For a while I *did* succeed in turning the other cheek – with the help of pills and vodka. That changed when the others came.

Now working hand in hand with the Devil, the two conspired to draw in others for the sake of Mammon. Like swarms of flies they arrived, buzzing through my home, to gorge themselves on her oozing, naked flesh. Each evening, when the last of the swarm left, slaked and bloated, the pair of them unashamedly counted out their filthy lucre on the kitchen table. They then celebrated, the only way they knew how, atop the table among the pestilence-stricken notes and coins. You would have imagined that even the Devil must sometimes tire of excessive indulgence in fetid fornication.

The temptation to shut down the world and choose forever the night was colossal. A handful of pills and I could escape in my sleep. I had wonderful visions of being welcomed into Paradise. In the place of pain and suffering – perpetual springtime. A place filled with brightness and birth, budding flowers and laughing babies. But then the Light was infiltrated by an enormous grey shadow that swallowed up the sky. The flowers wilted and decayed, the laughing babies grew pointed canines, turned black, sprouted tails and moved about on cloven hooves.

That I should succumb to the ultimate sin against the Light was part of her scheming. But just as I realised her strategy in time to sabotage her twisted plans, I was confined to my bed with a sudden illness that left me enervated and begging for death. Miraculously, I pulled through on the seventh day. The significance of my recovery on the symbolic seventh penetrated like the first hammer blow pounding home a bolt into one of my outstretched hands. I had a purpose, a true mission, and a reason for being: to beat the Devil at his own game.

Careful consideration brought me to a conclusion that, initially, I found impossible to accept, but which steadily washed through me for what it was: an irrefutable truth. My husband was completely blameless for everything that had taken and was taking place between him and the abomination masquerading as my daughter. What good man stood a chance when pitted against the greatest evil? My role was to rend the Devil's mask asunder, divest him of his cloak. Only then would my husband regain his purity and learn again to see the ugliness and deceit that lay hidden beneath seeming beauty.

The Devil made a mistake when he chose to inhabit the thirteen-year-old body of a fragile girl. Stripping her, for me, was easy. Watching the welts rise and the white skin bruise red and purple as I beat her, firstly with my fists and feet, and then with the back of the wooden hairbrush until the handle snapped, sent a flurry of excited sparks shooting and ricocheting from my stomach to my head. Her screams and pleas for me to stop, and the way she curled her skinny arms around her brazen body, where she lay twisted in the bleeding earth, was putrid animal fat tossed onto hungry flames.

"No, Mommy. Please, I'm sorry, Mommy," the thing whimpered in a perfect take of my daughter's voice.

"Begone Satan," I said, working the syllables to the rhythm of the blows I rained upon her. "Beelzebub," I went. "Lord of the Flies."

Her evil green eyes were petrified at having been rumbled for who she, he, it really was.

It was my turn next to endure punches and blows when he came in from work and found his chattel spoiled. Outwardly the wreck of a pubescent human being, she lay trembling on the couch where I had bundled her, having dragged her living carcass in from the back garden where she'd tasted the beginning stages of my retribution.

Everything continued then as I had foreseen it. From where he stood in the living-room doorway, freeze-framed, his incredulous eyes, rounded and horrified, telescoped onto the blackened and blood-caked mass of battered flesh. It seemed minutes, but was probably only seconds, before he tore his gaze from her to me. I closed my Bible and placed it reverently on the coffee table next to my armchair and allowed the joy washing through me to break across my face in a smile. It had been so long since last I felt so filled with bliss and goodness.

He reached me with such speed he might have been carried on the wings of angels.

"Yes. Yes," I said through the dazzling flashes of light that came with each successive knuckle crack against my jaw and face. I had finally reached him. The pain from the beating was as nothing compared to the knowledge that the man I was joined to in Holy Matrimony had taken his first steps on the journey away from evil.

The combination of our weight, together with the increased ferocity of his attack, tipped the armchair backwards and left us sprawled upon the floor, reunited lovers in a deathly embrace. The heat and rising scent, a burnt-umber manly smell, humming from his closeness, and the intimacy throbbing from his squeezing fingers wrapped around my throat, delivered me to a state so glorious, so divine, he must have seen the look of ecstasy in my face.

I clearly passed out for a while, for I next remember my demisting senses grasping that I was reseated in the righted armchair. Across from me in the opposite armchair, he sat resignedly, his eyes locked onto the stained carpet. His face now wore the expression of a man who has had the greatest of all wonders thrust upon him.

Too sore to get my body to carry out my divine impulses for a number of days, I, like Job, waited until I was ready to continue my Crusade. My husband's absence facilitated my mission – he left that day he saw the Light, and has yet to return. Sometimes the truth is too enormous and needs contemplation to fully accept what is put before the senses. He'll be back. This I know. I'll be here for him.

It's surprising how much the human body, even that of a thirteen-year-old girl, can withstand: being tied naked to a leafless tree beneath a clear moonlit sky on a freezing night in January, being constantly beaten with a rolling pin, a diet for three days of foul meat, and repeated suffocation with a plastic bag to the point where the deprivation of oxygen turns the face blue.

Although he, the Lord of the Flies, tries to convince me otherwise, with his girlie-pleas to me as his mother, my faith has kept me strong and rational. After all, what ordinary child, a child who hasn't been infested by demons, could survive for so long such extreme efforts at exorcism?

The past few evenings have brought with them the return of the misguided mortals swarming ravenously around my doorstep. For the sanctity of my marriage and the sake of my daughter's soul, He has bestowed on me the strength and courage required to counter this locust plague. While she lies broken-boned, gagged and bound in the wooden barrel at the end of the garden, I close my eyes and pray as the locusts feast upon my offered flesh.

The Day of Judgement is nigh. No sacrifice is too great, no suffering too painful, for a wife and mother with the might of God to guide her along the path of righteousness.

Amen.

That Man's Father

The racket from the little scumbags kicking a ball around outside tore away the refuge of sleep. Doc's head felt like it was clogged with gunk or some crap. But the gunk was no cushion against the bouncing ball and scumbag shouts and bellows. Felt like they were playing a match inside his head, the little bastards.

Straight out he knew he'd have to take something. Or he'd be really sick. But there was nothing in the gaff. He'd have to buzz up into town. Sharp-like. Luckily, it shouldn't take too long. That's why he liked living in the city centre.

Lifting the dirty, off-white duvet away from over his covered head, he sat up, kept his eyes closed against the daylight blazing through the curtainless window, leaned forward and worked his hand around the floor to locate by touch his socks, which he pressed to his nose – they passed the sniff test.

Gradually he allowed the day to enter his eyes, firstly by opening his eyelids the width of a splinter, and then fully when he put on his fake Ray-Bans. Next he pulled on his white tracksuit.

Now he was ready. Before thumbing the redial key on his mobile, he worked his fingers under his sunglasses and scraped the sleep from his eyes with his blackened fingernails.

The voice on the end of the line was gruff and sounded pissed-off.

"I know," Doc said. "I know. I have you. But, it's an emergency, man. I don't have nothing like."

Without mentioning names or locations, they agreed to hook up in the usual place at eleven bells. Doc then snapped his phone shut and left the flat.

"Morning Doc," one of the two women said as he

passed them at the bottom of the stairwell that led up to his and their flats.

"Ah, hello, missus," he said. "How are we doing?" He could never get their names anymore.

"That's a grand day for you now," the second one said. "Nice and sunny for you now. Look it." And she waved her arm in a sweeping arc at the sky behind her.

"Thanks," Doc said. "Thanks, missus."

They always managed to make themselves sound better than him. '… a grand day for you now'. Like they were the ones giving him the day. A pair of old wagons.

The advancing bus, the shrinking figure and the hurrying pedestrians couldn't deny it: the man, now partially concealed in the crowd, had the same stooped posture, the identical checked sports-jacket; and the way he paused to rest against a shop front, the walking stick tucked under his arm – even the same shuffling steps. It had to be. It was. Couldn't be anybody else: Colm's dead father.

But, how could it be him? Colm had kissed his old man's forehead, as cold as marble, the day of the funeral; the first and last time he'd pressed his lips to his father's face. He'd brushed back the soggy hair from his own forehead and watched the torrential rain drum roll off the small, mucky puddles that had formed round the gaping black hole at the graveside, the water flowing in thin channels into the unwelcoming wound in the earth.

And yet, maybe, just maybe. But maybe what? Colm didn't know what to think or consider.

He twisted round in the bus seat to look after the elderly man in the street. The man's face had been the face Colm's father had worn in his final years. "Sorry. Excuse me," Colm said to the young woman who smelled of jasmine sitting next to him, as he felt himself rising to get off at the next stop, three or four stops before his.

Since his retirement, Alfie and his wife Mags enjoyed Tuesday as their special day out together. Up early and into town on the Luas, a full Irish breakfast in the Kylemore, a stroll around the shops, under no time pressures to be anywhere else, and up as far as the Green to feed the ducks if the weather was fine, a light lunch in Bewley's café and home before four. Lovely.

This ritual Alfie continued after Mags had gone into hospital. Her lovely, chubby face swelled with interest and excitement on those Tuesday afternoon visits when he described to her what some chap, a gas character, known well to him and Mags had done or said in Henry Street.

"And did you have the Full Irish?" she'd ask him, or "What's going into the ground this weather, love, up on the Green?"

But those Tuesday visits were few. Mags was admitted to hospital at the end of February and had passed on by early April.

For over a year since Mags's passing, Alfie kept up the Tuesday morning trips into the city. At first he talked to Mags in his head. He heard her voice comment on what a beautiful day it was. *Sure isn't everyday a beautiful day so long as you're in it?* he'd say as well. And he'd hear her big happy laugh crowding the morning, as honest and pure as the hidden blackbirds singing in the trees and bushes.

A few months after Mags's death, Alfie graduated to talking to his dead wife aloud, left a pause for her response, and laughed with her, nodding his head in casual greeting at the people in the street who smiled at him. He accepted the smiles for the two of them, he and Mags, the way they used to be: an aging couple, still happy together and there for each other at a time in life when they depended so much upon the other's support.

"Doc. Doc," one of the lads called to him from a third floor balcony.

Jayzus, he couldn't even get out of the bleeding complex.

Doc stopped, turned round and squinted up and through the sizzling daylight. He chucked his chin up at the youth. "Alright?'

"Hold up, Doc. I'm coming down."

"What's the story?" Doc said to the other's retreating back. You had to look after your customers, no matter what.

The youth disappeared into his flat and emerged quickly through the door at the bottom of the stairwell.

Doc knew exactly what the other wanted. He had to stop him before he got going.

"Haven't got nothing," Doc said, before the youth reached him. He held out his arms like the statue of your man in O'Connell Street. "I don't have nothing. I've got to blast off to see a man, like. Alright?"

"I know how you mean," the youth said. "Game-ball. I'll catch you later then, Doc."

"Sound," Doc replied.

Doc pulled his tracksuit hood up over his head before he reached the young fellows taking penalties in the vandalised basketball court, their goalposts constructed from a bent and flattened traffic cone and a burnt, blackened and melted car seat.

"Nay, what's up, Doc?" the bigger of them shouted at him, in his usual, nasally impression of Bugs Bunny. The rest of them exploded into laughter, like they always did.

"Fuck off, you little pox-bottles," Doc said. Just wait another few years and they were old enough. He'd fucking show them who they were messing with. Fucking pox-bottles.

Catching up to the old man was easier than Colm had expected. He hadn't got far. The elderly man, the man he had yet to be convinced wasn't his dead father, might even have been waiting for him. Colm slowed his pace before he drew near, glancing at his watch as some kind of diversion.

Another half hour and they'd be arriving in the office. Colm would phone in and tell them he'd be late, he considered it, but, really, his decision was already made. He wouldn't be going in at all today.

Alfie's walking stick clattering to the pavement was what did it. No break came in the parade of legs. And when he stooped, in an attempt to retrieve the stick, the shooting pain caught him as though someone had rammed a blade into his lower spine. Despite the pain, he forced himself to twist round and face the shopfront window, lest the passers-by see him whinging and blubbering like an old fool.

"Christ, the pain, love," he said aloud, as though Mags were next to him. "Me back is gone again."

"Don't you worry none," he heard Mags say. "We'll get a nice cup of tea and a scone in the Kylemore. Again we get back home, the pain'll have eased off. Like before."

Mags was right. She was always right.

"Are you alright, mister," a young man's voice asked.

Startled at being rumbled in such a pitiful state, at the same time, Alfie could feel himself coming completely undone. He kept his head down, his hand covering his face.

Into his other hand was placed the familiar wooden walking stick, a gift from Mags.

There you go," the young man said. "Nothing to worry about. Now, are you okay?"

Alfie tucked his head further into his chest, sucking up the increased pain. He nodded that he was fine, but felt his entire body racking, as the tears he could no longer control burned his eyes. And then it hit him. Like being clobbered from behind, it was. What was he doing? Why was he here? What reason was there to come into town on Tuesdays anymore? Mags was gone. He'd sat with her in the hospital ward that last day, gripping her limp hand until it felt like a piece of unwrapped chicken taken from the fridge. She ended. A fact he had known but rejected. He was left on his own. Alone. A temporary error that would be corrected once he too ended.

The unexpected touch and warmth of a human hand pressed against his upper back made Alfie look up and squint at the reflection in the shop-front window. The young man, his saviour, a bit rough looking, wore a hood that made it difficult to see his face.

Doc said that was game-ball with him. He'd love to join the old boy for some grub. In fact, he hadn't had any breakfast and could really go for some toast and a cuppa. Except, and he told the old man he was sorry for saying it and the whole lot. But he'd left his wallet back in his gaff. He was stony he was.

"Never you mind, son," the old man said. "It's on me. Sure what would an auld fella like me be doing with me money anyway?"

The laugh Doc shared with the old man made his head feel as if the backs of his eyeballs was the wall the little scumbags used as the net they measured out between their makeshift goalposts, and at which they were pounding quickfire penalties.

"What ails you, son?" the old man asked. "Is it sick you are or what?"

"No, no," Doc said, pinching the bridge of his nose. "It's just headaches. Me head is bursting."

The old man said he might have a few Aspro in his pocket, only his back was hurting too much for the moment to go hunting for them. He told Doc to dip right in and dig them out. The tablets were in a little blue box, he told him.

"Are you sure?" Doc asked. "I mean I don't want to be rooting around your stuff and the whole lot."

"Go right ahead, son, please."

Fumbling in the old man's pocket, the old man's smell was stronger: A sour smell that reminded Doc of his ma's aunt – a comforting smell.

It should have been him. The guy in the tracksuit got to him first. But who was this guy? What did he want with the old man? Broken images of the time Colm's father came home, the evening he'd been jumped by a gang of drunken teenagers, his swollen eye, eggplant purple, and the dark-red blood already congealing under his father's nose formed and faded in Colm's head.

If this guy so much as touched the old man…

Colm took out his mobile and affected taking a call.

With the phone pressed to his ear, he mumbled and nodded, moving slowly after the pair, each looking sicker than the other, as they threaded through the crowd in the direction of the Green. The way the younger man supported the old man, his arm around his waist and the old man's arm draped round the younger's shoulder had Colm guessing they were father and son. They were even laughing together, the type of laughter that belonged to the street, laughter loud and spontaneous, like the combined wingbeats of a startled flock of pigeons.

What an idiot he'd been. Impulsively getting off the bus and missing work to stalk an old man who happened to be the image of his dead father. He laughed aloud and pretended to speak to somebody on the phone.

What an asshole.

Now he'd have to lay low and hang about town till after five. There were always too many officials connected to the office, on supposed business, moving about town; he'd bumped into them often on his days off. They were a bunch of big mouths.

But hang on. Did he see what he thought he just saw? The guy in the hoodie had stopped, manoeuvred himself so that he and the old man were facing each other and, with his fingers pressing the bridge of his nose, as though he was supposed to be dizzy or something, had dipped his hand into the old man's coat pocket.

Colm slipped his mobile into its leather cover, shoved it into his trousers' pocket, and took off after the pair like a lioness locked onto a potential kill.

"Watch where you're going, you gobshite, you," a guy Colm accidently collided with said.

"Sorry," Colm said over his shoulder, offering an apologetic wave.

"You moron, you," the guy shouted.

Resisting the impulse to spin round and shout after the prick that he'd said 'Sorry' to, Colm pushed on, an urge to slam his hands into the shoulders of the next prick that got in his way tearing at the inside of his stomach. There was nothing that pissed him off more than when you apologised to some prick and he acted as though you hadn't said 'Sorry'.

Already Alfie's back pain was easing off. Once he got himself sitting down, he'd be grand. Especially if there was one of the longer seats free in the Kylemore, he could kind of lean sideways and rest on his elbow.

"Banjaxed," he said to the young man. "The pair of us is banjaxed, what?"

The two men laughed.

"We'll be right as rain soon as we take a load off and grab a bit of brekkie," the young man said.

Alfie rubbed his hands together, and then raised up his arms. He flinched with the pain.

"In me inside pocket there's me wallet. Reach in and dig it out, son, will you?"

"You sure?"

Alfie nodded hard to convince the young man of his trust, the sudden movement of his head causing the invisible dagger to catch his lower back with another thrust. He drew in a sharp breath and consciously tried to turn the spreading fire in his spine into a joke.

"The tea and scones isn't going to pay for themselves, is it?" he said, his own attempt at laughter sounding more like a whine. Jesus, he had to sit down quick. He felt himself stumbling and, if not for the young man, he would have... well, he wasn't sure what he would have; his head wasn't working too good.

Doc's eyes refused to focus and he needed to open his belt. He fumbled in the old man's wallet, failing to push through the sudden, sickening dizziness that almost made him trip at the top of the escalator.

"I have you," the old man said. "Take it handy, son. We're nearly there."

"Thanks," Doc said. "It's me head. I just need to get a load off, you know?" He allowed the old man to take his weight as they struggled through the café entrance and towards their seats. Black and red shutters wavered before him, clouding his vision.

Colm followed the pair into the shopping centre. Suddenly the roles seemed to have been reversed. The hoody somehow looked as if he were now the one being supported by the old man. They took the escalator, the older man helping the younger onto the first step in a practised manner. Colm stayed eight or nine steps behind them.

There, he was right. The hoody now had his hand stuck into the old man's inside pocket, the older man's pained, though laughing face, was nodding like a horse.

Threatening him. That's what he was at.

Although too far from them to hear the hoody's whispered threats, Colm had him sussed. He knew his type. Looked like he was even getting the old man to laugh, as if everything was normal.

A believer in destiny, Colm experienced an instantaneous sense of who he was and what he was for. Of all the thousands of early morning shoppers and people on their way to work, Colm alone saw what others could not see.

Soon as they sat down in the roundy central seat, the lad conked out. Poor chap. Sleeping. He was kind of half-lying against the imitation leather backrest and half-propped up against Alfie. Through the closeness and warmth of the lad's body, Alfie felt the quickened breathing of the sleeping young man, the way he used to feel Mags's breathing when she slept next to him those cold winter nights in the bed they'd shared for over forty years.

Not wanting to disturb the young man, Alfie remained as he was until his left arm, wedged between them, grew so numb it felt like it had disappeared and been replaced by the young man pressed to his side.

Carefully, Alfie supported the other by the shoulder using his free hand, leaned slightly away from him, and worked his trapped arm free. Used to this kind of deadness in his limbs and how to deal with it, he needed to smack his arm against his thigh to get some blood flowing through it. That could wait. Instead he left it draped round the young man's shoulders, closed his eyes and did what he always did: walked arm in arm in his head with Mags through Dublin's thronging streets in early spring and on into summertime, or when the Christmas lights, sparkling overhead, crowded the day with holiness and filled the vendors' voices with a kind of godliness that made Mags wipe the corners of her eyes with her linen handkerchief and laugh at her own foolishness.

"That's my girl," Alfie would say, stopping in the street and pulling her to him in an effort to hide the emotion he felt suffusing his own face. "You're the best girl ever was."

Doc felt the buzzing in his tracksuit bottoms' pocket before he was fully conscious. Into his nostrils came a stale urinary hum that played through the buzzing and wove its way into the familiar thudding beat of Coolio's *Gangsta's Paradise*. His phone, his bleeding phone was ringing. But he couldn't move. And his eyes wouldn't open. He was fucking paralysed. Jesus fucking Christ, he was bollixed. And where the fuck was he? And who the fuck had his arm around his neck and the other in his lap? Whoever it was smelled like a piss-alley. Fuck.

By the time Colm had got his coffee, paid for it and sat himself at a table near them, the pair seemed to be asleep in each other's arms. This was getting weirder.

Colm scanned the other customers. Apart from a middle-aged suit eating a bowl of something while devouring The Irish Times, and a young woman with yellow hair touching up her make-up in a hand-held mirror, the place was quite empty.

Working his way out from the chair at his table by the window and approaching the two seemingly sleeping men, Colm experienced the strange sensation of watching the scene as though from the eyes of someone else's dream.

Asleep, his mouth open, exposing off-white, gangly teeth, the old man looked even more like Colm's father. With no idea what he was going to do or say, he leaned forward and tapped the old man on the shoulder.

"Excuse me, sir."

A funny sound bubbled in the old man's throat, but his eyes remained closed and he kind of pulled the hoody closer to him, as if he was protecting him.

Colm straightened up, scratched his head and twisted his torso sideways to glance at the suit and the yellow-haired woman. Neither of them was paying him any attention. "Dad. Dad," he heard himself whisper next to the old man's ear. The man breathed heavily but stayed asleep.

Colm then sidled around the small square table, fighting the shaky feeling in his legs, clenched his teeth and prodded the hoody once in the shoulder.

"Hey. Excuse me." No reaction. He looked harder at him. The hoody didn't even seem to be breathing. He prodded him again, this time with three fingers, using greater conviction. "Hey you, muppet. What are you up to, motherfucker?" Calling him 'motherfucker' emboldened Colm, made him feel like Pacino or De Niro dealing with some dirtbag in a movie. He scrutinised the hoody's face: sunken cheeks, eyes too close, a long nose and a lipless gash for a mouth – features all squashed together to present the type of face that always soured the contents of Colm's stomach when he passed them on the street.

Scattered images of Colm's father's terrifying and terrified countenance staring out from behind a mask of swellings, bruises and blackened-blood flickered about in his head.

One punch. Colm knew the system. As a civil servant he was part of it. By the time a Garda arrived he'd be long gone. One swift punch to the jugular would do it. These muppets targeting old men like his father. No respect for nobody. Let them claw at their own throats as their filthy lungs gasped for life.

He was going down the fucking tubes. That was the bad shit. He had to have taken some bad shit. Doc felt fully alert now, sort of. But his body was frozen and his eyes were stitched closed. He remembered coming into the Kylemore with the old boy. But why in the name of fuck was the old man wrapped around him like a fucking rollie?

"Excuse me, sir," someone said.

What the—? Who was that – the manager or somebody?

"Dad. Dad," the voice went on in a whisper. The auld fella's son?

Doc heard the old man's 'son' moving about. He could feel the vibrations on the floor through his feet.

Shite. The pox-bottle had just prodded him. "Hey," the voice went. "Excuse me." Doc felt himself being jabbed again, only now it felt like the pox-bottle meant business. "Hey you, muppet. What are you up to, motherfucker?"

Doc didn't like fucking nobody laying a finger on him; didn't matter who the fuck he was.

His blade. He had to get his blade out, but his Jayzus hands just wouldn't fucking work. And behind his eyes the balls were now slamming like they were being fired from a bleeding cannon… but wait. His eyes were coming unstuck – and his fingers – he could wiggle his fingers.

Straight out he knew how to handle things. His

stomach. His stomach told him exactly what he had to do. He'd play unconscious. Let the pox-bottle think he had the upper hand, and then let him have it. Bam.

Colm was startled by the appearance from nowhere of the uniformed guy who sidled up beside him.

He held up his hands as though he were a bank teller with a gun pointed at his face from behind protective glass. "No," he said, shaking his head and before the security guy, a little ape without a neck, spoke. "It's this guy." He indicated the hoody. "He's up to something. Trying to rob my… I mean, look at him. He's up to no good… Hey, what are you…?"

The ape had locked his huge paw onto Colm's collar and was shaking his head. "I've been watching you."

"Don't touch me, you prick," Colm heard himself saying in a voice that sounded like someone else's voice. And he felt himself slamming the ape hard in the shoulders with his palms. A mistake. He might as well have slammed his hands into an oak. Except the oak tree wouldn't have been able to grab Colm by the arm, flip him round the way you might a naughty child, and twist his arm up his back until the pain felt so great he fell to the floor.

"Get off me," Colm roared. "Jesus, my arm. Please, get off me."

"Take it easy, Scobie," the ape said. "Okay? Just take it easy."

Colm felt the burning in his shoulder easing, but being replaced by a fire in the crooks of his knees, across which the ape was now half-kneeling.

"Mags," Alfie whispered through the threatening shouts, loaded with violence. Violence had always terrified her. "Don't worry, love. It'll pass." And he pulled her closer to him. But the shouting grew louder. And there was music, the type of music from one of those disturbing movies. And her smell; Mags suddenly didn't smell like Mags. And she felt wrong.

The shouting voices dragged Alfie back into a world where Mags no longer existed.

"Mags," Alfie shouted, pushing the sickly-smelling young fellow from him. "Help me, Mags. Help."

Through half-lidded eyes, Doc watched the pox-bottle being throttled, and a toasty feeling came into his stomach, which worked its way upward and made his head buzz. Like the feeling you got with good gear. The sound of Coolio's *Gangsta's Paradise* starting up again in his pocket came in as though on cue, the way it did in those flicks when the guy everyone treated like a punk showed them he was 'The Man'. Deadly.

High Flyer

Most of all Isabel noticed his hands. They were good hands, dark-skinned, kind hands, but capable, too. It took huge effort during the twenty-minute journey home not to glance directly at his face again. When the sound of the engine shifted, as the train roared through the short tunnels, she watched his window reflection watching hers.

And now they were about to get off at the same station. He was standing so close behind her, she could smell his after shave: a musky manly smell. The awareness of his inadvertent breath caressing the back of her neck caused a tingling sensation to ripple through her.

The doors whooshed open and she and the other passengers spilled out. Isabel darted a few paces along the platform, as though she were late for an appointment. She then stopped and fumbled for her phone. An excuse to look at him without appearing to do so.

The man from the train carriage looked at her too as he walked by. She saw his eyes slide over her chest and down to her legs, then slide back up to her face. He sort of smiled.

Isabel remembered this type of look from men. Almost. A look they pretended you weren't supposed to notice but made quite sure you did. A look she couldn't remember inspiring for years, not since before she and Don had yet to find each other. Long before Robert existed.

This got Isabel thinking about it all again. The way Don broke the news to her that evening five months ago when they came home from Sweden. How he was leaving her the house, and how, financially, she and Robert would never have to worry about a thing. He'd see to it. He was even giving Robert his car when Don's own car, the very latest model, arrived from Germany.

Once she'd gotten past the screaming and recrimination,

she heard herself sounding like a clichéd-abandoned wife. After twenty years. What had she done? What could another woman give him that she couldn't? Hadn't she always been a loving wife to him and a good mother to Robert?

He was sorry. He really was, but she'd thank him in years to come. He knew she would.

Bastard.

That morning, the first day back at school after the summer break, Justin had trudged through the streets with his skateboard tucked under his armpit. On the ground the fallen leaves were wet and sad, and the wind blew the rain into his face and drenched his uniform. By the time the bell rang to go home after lunch, the rain had stopped, his clothes were dry, and the sun made everything bright and yellow.

Bombing along the footpath on his skateboard, Justin felt giddy, a little light-headed, though in control. The way he sometimes felt when he and his friends listened to The Game, his favourite rap singer. He was racing the bus between stops and mostly winning. On the bus were some girls he knew to see from school. With his cool sunglasses on, he pretended he didn't notice them waving and laughing to get his attention. He imagined his own face looking cool and tough, wearing the look he had practised at home in the mirror.

Weaving their way among the images of himself were fractured thoughts of the lads in school telling him that his new haircut was 'deadly'. He ran his fingertips through his close-cropped hair, and crouched, readying himself for a kerb.

The guy in the car next to Robert's tried to pull across him. No indication. He floored it. The guy swerved back into his own lane. A 1999 D Golf. Red.

In the rear-view mirror Robert watched the moron's car shrinking. A swelling sense of joy washed through him. He burst into operatic gibberish, imitating the Bocelli C.D. playing on his stereo, and laughed at the sound of his voice straining to land on the high notes.

Finally. He had one. A black BMW convertible. A gift from his father – what a gift. And he had just turned nineteen. The break-up between his mom and dad no longer seemed as crushing as it had been these past months.

He climbed down the gears at the sight of a couple of women wheeling strollers in the distance. Always worth a look. Bingo. Yummy-mummies.

That's when the moron in the Golf whizzed past. The driver held down the horn and waved his arm out the window and above the car roof. A wuss's wave.

Robert stabbed off the stereo and shifted from fourth to sixth. He caught him at the lights. They were side by side. Peripherally, he could see the guy giving him the finger and pretending to laugh, as though he were better than him.

"Get out of the car," Robert mouthed, and indicated that he'd snap him in half. The guy kept doing what he was doing.

Robert felt himself getting out of the car, even though he didn't want to. The lights changed. Relief.

The moron got away first. He caught him easily and zoomed past. Ahead, another set of lights. Amber. Robert slowed down and then speeded up on red.

Isabel made a conscious effort not to open the doors to all the rooms in the house when she got home. A ritual she'd carried out every day since he'd left her. Had she really expected him to be back home, waiting for her with diamonds and roses, saying what a mistake he'd made, and what a fool he was to have been blinded for a while by some money-hungry little floozy? Yes. She had.

Isabel poured herself a glass of wine, downed it in one gulp, poured another and took it and the bottle with her to the bedroom. Before peeling off the skirt suit she'd worn to the interview for a change of job, she studied in the wardrobe mirror how the young man on the train must have seen her. Standing akimbo, she used her eyes the way she'd been trained to in photo shoots as a young woman. It wasn't about pouting, showing teeth or running a glistening tongue over moist lips. The eyes. The eyes were what drew men in and captured them. Even if, or especially if, they didn't know it.

Not bad for thirty-nine. And who could possibly imagine she had a nineteen-year-old son? Isabel could understand a young man getting excited and disturbed by the way she looked. She began to undress slowly, holding the gaze of the invisible young man for whom she was removing her clothing.

Justin cleared the kerb smoothly and mounted the other one as though his board grew out of him. He could see the girls on the bus clapping his cool move as the bus wheeled on by. Who else had seen him? Up ahead there was somebody, a tiny old woman at fifty paces, but she was shaking her walking stick at him. He slowed down and freewheeled for a bit then stamped down on the back of the board, dismounted, and snatched it up.

As he and the old woman drew closer, he noticed her mouth moving but he couldn't hear any words. Her head looked as though it had shrunk maybe in the rain, and there were far more stripes on her face than on his granny's face. She looked about a hundred. Justin was readying himself and his board to shove off after the bus, when the old woman's claw grabbed him by the jumper.

"Get off me. Leave us alone, missus."

The old woman's walking stick clattered to the ground and she had him with both claws. She clung to him like Whiskers McGrath, his neighbour's cat, and her round eyes through huge glasses were crazy. She smelled sour. "The priest. Do you want to come over to see the priest?"

"What are you on about?" Justin said, feeling something banging from inside his chest. "I just want to go home." He pulled free from the old woman, swiped up his board and sped off, only realizing that he was crying when he saw the bus stopped up ahead at the traffic lights.

He wiped the corners of his eyes with the grey sleeves of his school uniform jumper and prepared for a really sharp move. He built up the necessary speed by tearing along the path using his left foot. At the pedestrian lights he leaned sideways, his arms outstretched like aircraft wings, and hooked around the traffic light pole and onto the road. He jumped slightly to clear the low kerb onto the traffic island, all the time aware that the girls were watching his performance from the upstairs deck of the bus.

Robert turned his head pointedly to sneer at the moron coming to a stop in the left lane. Amber lights were for idiots. They let them know their station. Idiots couldn't function if they weren't told what to do. For Robert, a high-flying soon-to-be young executive when he finished college, amber lights meant lowering speed and climbing down a gear in readiness to drive faster.

The speed made Robert's tyres screech horribly before he hit the boy that had come from nowhere on the skateboard.

With a couple more glasses of wine in her while she soaked in the bathtub, Isabel was in a relaxed and drowsy state, thinking, or dreaming perhaps, about the encounter with the young man on the train when the phone rang in the bedroom. She let it ring out. If it were important they'd ring again. They did.

Reluctantly she climbed out of the tub, draped her dressing gown over her shoulders and padded into the bedroom. "Yes, hello?"

"There's been an accident."

"What? Robert, is that you? What did you say?"

Robert's voice was panicky and the line was breaking up. In the background she could hear voices and the sound of traffic.

"Where are you? Are you okay?"

Robert said he wasn't sure. "Near where that old church is, you know the one?"

"Ask somebody. Do you hear me, Robert? Ask somebody where you are. Robert? Robert?" She took the hand set away from her head and stared at it, then pressed it back to her ear. "Robert?" The line was dead.

In her first attempt to call him back, she couldn't get her shaking fingers right and must have hit a wrong button. A woman's voice answered. Isabel slammed the phone down on the hook. The second time she dialled his number she got through to his voicemail greeting. "Robert, listen to me," she said after the tone, but didn't go on. He was probably trying to reach her.

While she dragged onto her wet body the dirty clothes she'd earlier removed, she was fighting the idea of calling Don, when Robert called again. He couldn't stay on for long, but told her what had happened. She listened carefully to the name of the hospital where the policeman told him they were taking the boy. Robert himself would get there as soon as the police were finished with him. He thought they were taking the car, too. Abruptly, he told her he had to go. “Don’t worry, Mom.” He added that he loved her.

Robert had yet to arrive when Isabel made it to the hospital by taxi. At reception in Accident and Emergency, she learned that nobody was permitted to see the boy who had been knocked down. She seated herself in the waiting room, and scanned the unhappy faces, wanting to, and not wanting to, locate the injured boy’s parents. She couldn’t.

The sound of a woman’s hysterical screams above other voices drew her into the corridor. Three men, one a priest, were struggling to restrain a woman who was wailing and smashing her head off the wall. The successive blows of the woman’s head pounding the wall reverberated inside Isabel’s chest.

Of Men and Dogs

"Lie down, Amadeus," the man said, and gave the animal a kind of shoving kick or kicking shove in the ribs with his boot.

The ancient Irish Wolfhound, over a hundred in dog years, raised a sad eyebrow and then cowered arthritically back into its corner, where it eased itself, with a doggy sigh, onto its dirty blanket.

"I'm sorry, old pal," he said, while working his way around the never-used baby grand piano. He ran his fingers from the dog's head into its wiry-furred back.

Amadeus shuddered but otherwise ignored him.

The dog, adored by the man's father, whom the dog had worshipped in return, almost tolerated, and was tolerated by the man.

"I miss him, too."

And it was true. Nine months on since his father last cursed him, he did miss him. What was, at first, the release he'd been awaiting for two years, two years spent tending to his father's every need, along with the constant whims and demands – the expensive Italian wines and daily, fresh-baked bread, the weekly hassle with taxis and the wheelchair on those trips to the theatre and the cinema; and, worst of all, that constant jangling bell summoning him from sleep to carry his father into the bathroom on his countless imagined urges throughout the night – all this had lately triggered in the man a longing ache.

Only now, in the past few weeks, did the reality that his father had truly ended become an undeniable fact. In the initial months, in springtime, his father's death didn't affect him. He occupied himself as he had always done at that time of year. He busied himself in the garden. He worked through the stabbing pain in his lower back, a condition brought on, he guessed, from carrying his father's frail body up and down the narrow stairs three or four times a day, for days that ran into hundreds.

In the garden there were always necessary jobs to be done – the plague of buttercups and nettles made no concessions for pain. There were rosebushes to be pruned, and fruit bushes to be cut back. The compressed and choking earth was in need of turning. Seedlings, already potted in the glasshouse, had to be nursed into larger pots before transplanting to prepared vegetable patches and flowerbeds.

At night-time, whilst reaping the reward and relief his orthopaedic mattress brought his chronic back pain, he rewound the day's gardening in his head. He then planned the work yet to be done, his mind's eye preparing a meticulous imaginary palette creating the different stages that would lead to a garden bursting with character and colour.

Never had a dream been so surpassed. The heady fragrance released by the carpet of jasmine, which attracted miniature, powder-blue butterflies, set off a humming chorus as bee swarms worked the tiny flowers. Woven through the buzzing background, birdsong dripped from the heavily-laden plum trees, whose fruit was healthily pink and swelled with juice.

Early autumn now, the bees had gone and the fruit lay bleeding and dying in the exhausted earth. Nothing to be done. The man woke up nights imagining he'd heard the manic jingle-jangling of his father's small, hand-held bell calling him. A non-believer, he had a vague recollection of hearing something about bereavement hallucinations. He wondered how he'd react were his father's ghostly image to appear before him sitting at the end of his bed. But his father stayed away.

The man nonetheless steeled himself, pulled himself from sleep in the early hours, got out of bed and went into his father's bedroom, convinced he would see his father and hear his groans as surely as he expected he would not.

The man's own weeping surprised him, but then became a constant. Often he realised he'd been blubbering softly, like some ancient widow, without hardly being aware of when he began or what the trigger was that brought it on. And yet, the father he mourned had been responsible for what the man recognised as the ruination of his life. It began long before the crippling illness took hold two years ago. Fourteen, almost fifteen years back, not long after his father's retirement. The time the man's mother passed away marked the time when the foundations on which his future was erected began to disintegrate.

The telegram in which the man learned of his mother's sudden death undermined the roots he had carefully planted and nurtured in America. Seven years he had toiled on the building sites in the States, and had moved beyond the initial stages required in the setting up of his own building firm.

"I'll hang myself," his father threatened, when the man finally announced his plan to depart after putting off his return to the States three months since his mother's funeral. "On your conscience be it. Your own father." How was he supposed to take care of himself? "I'll slit my throat," he continued, drawing his thumb across his neck.

The man agreed to stick around for another few months, just until his father learned to adjust. "You'll get beyond this, Dad," he said. "I know it's hard right now. But, believe me, you'll get there."

Assisted by the State, the man supplemented his benefit income by doing the occasional brick laying job, though usually just as the established bricky's mate. Mixing cement, sweeping up, and swapping stories with the men who threw the odd job his way provided counterpoint to what was developing into a caring role to his father.

His father's steadily increasing drinking habit, which kept him in a permanent state of inebriation, relieved only by bouts of illness, together with his unpredictable behaviour, soon conspired to keep the man from accepting the sparse offers of work. His father couldn't be left unsupervised.

Among the less offensive of his father's new ways was his arriving at a neighbour's place with a bucket of water and cloth, which he used, unsolicited, to wash the car parked in the driveway. More disturbing were the times he entered local small-farmers' properties and worried the livestock with shouts and gesticulations. But positively outraging were the reports of how he urinated in public places: footpaths in the centre of town, outside the school, even one time against the large glass front of the town's only butcher's, behind which was displayed the meat on which the town's population depended. And then there was his dangerous predilection for crossing roads at a deliberate snail's-pace, challenging the halted driver with that stare, before lighting into a shouting rage if his goading challenge was taken up.

Once it seemed to be taken as read by the man and his father that the man had awoken from his American Dream and found it no more than just that, an impossible fantasy, then his father's idiosyncratic ways died down.

But whenever the man's suspicions had him pondering the extent to which his father had played on the notion that he was going a little dinky-donk – as they said in the States – lest he be completely deserted, the father topped his previous antics by howling at the moonless sky, or shuffling up the central aisle in church at ten o'clock mass on Sunday, having stripped to his underwear.

The arrival of the wolfhound puppy acted, for a while, as relief to the huge tension that had developed between the two men. Amadeus, the name his father gave the robust two-month-old dog, also became the marker that pinpointed the beginning of his father's extravagancies.

In the meantime, Amadeus, who the man's father insisted be given the run of the small cottage, treated the house and its contents as playthings. He gnawed the wooden legs of tables and chairs, chewed up cushions and ate whatever he considered edible and could reach whilst standing on his hind legs.

Soon Amadeus was the size of a small donkey, only more stubborn. The wolfhound commandeered the living room's most comfortable armchair, refused to be housetrained and, generally, was its own master. It slept where it wished: on the carpet just inside the front door, across the kitchen threshold, on the rubber mat in the bathroom, or stretched luxuriously on top of the blankets in the man's bed. The small house reeked of wet dog.

Between the young dog and the man's father there appeared to be an understanding. At mealtimes, the father addressed his sparse conversation to Amadeus, who sat upright next to the old man's chair, lending the aged father a ragged nobility. An impish look might come over the father's face, and with it, as though on cue, Amadeus would bound off about the house and hurl himself against some object hitherto unbroken or not yet battened down, a flower-pot stand or a coffee table.

The father, who shouted him down and cursed his lack of compassion for dumb animals and old men, countered the man's protestations and attempts to scold Amadeus. Only, the thing is, the man was convinced that Amadeus was no ordinary 'dumb animal'. The dog and the man's father were in cahoots against him, he had no doubt.

Why else would the ‘dumb animal’ fail to recognise the man and his scent those times when he was prevented from entering his father’s front gate with the morning bread? From inside the gate Amadeus snarled and frothed, chased his own tail, and gave the man a convincing warning that he’d tear him asunder should he get hold of him.

The man’s shouts to his father from outside the gate were ignored, even though he could make out his father’s watching figure behind the net curtains. The contented, vicious laughter rippling from his father’s throat was easy to imagine.

Like a herd of wild horses, the years galloped by. The father’s vindictive laughter was replaced by verbal onslaughts that left him enervated, and gave his face the incredulous stare of a man aware of his impending end. Amadeus’s ornery playfulness gave way to indifference. The dog’s rapid decline transformed Amadeus from a vital creature to a thing more decrepit than the diminished, wrinkled version of the man’s father.

The final sentiment bellowed at the man as he attempted to sponge-bathe his father in his dying bed was the old man’s favourite expletive. In those two words was contained the shadow of his father’s pride and strength as he raged against the crumbling quarter-light. His father’s dark eyes flicked open momentarily, regarded the man with glorious hatred, closed and never reopened.

Nine months on since that day his father had summarised his legacy to the man, in the seconds before he sucked in his last breath, it occurred to the man while petting Amadeus that the ailing wolfhound had replaced his father. He was thinking about getting himself back into the workforce. The cortisone treatment had eased his back problem immensely. As soon as he was one hundred percent, he vowed to himself that he'd put himself back on the market. He could sell the cottage – too many memories – and move into an apartment where there'd be no garden to tempt him. Of course he'd have to bring Amadeus to the vet. Have him put to sleep.

"No use to anyone anymore," he said to the outstretched wolfhound. He dragged his fingertips back up along Amadeus's spine and onto his head. "Not even any use to yourself now."

Amadeus's eyes blinked to life and locked onto the man's. He curled back his lips, exposing off-colour gums and yellowed teeth, his foul breath the stench of rotting vegetables. From the wolfhound's throat came a steady, pneumatic snarl before his eyelids slid over his black eyes.

"Amadeus."

The wolfhound's eyes reopened, attached themselves to the man's concerned face, and stayed open.

"Don't worry. I'll take care of you." His father wouldn't have expected less. Besides, there were daffodil and tulip bulbs he had to get into the earth for next spring before the frost.

On the Seventh Day

While Ellie scraped the razor down his cheekbone to his jaw, he tried to synchronise his breathing with hers. Her breath caressed his face. The nerve twitching at the side of his head pulled his reluctant eyes towards his own reflection in the bathroom mirror.

"I hate being awake," he said. "I can't make it through this."

"Yes you can," Ellie replied, dropping the razor into the dirty water. "Look at me." she cupped his half-shaved face in her hands and chased his retreating eyes with her bright stare. "You are not responsible." She landed on each syllable as though English was, for him, a foreign tongue.

"What do I say to that woman?" he asked. "And to the boy's father?"

"They forgive you. They're religious people. Their faith is so strong."

He didn't want forgiveness. He wanted condemnation. Punishment. To run through marshy land at night-time, an angry mob and baying hounds closing, until the pain ripped through his screaming lungs and he could go no farther, and the mob took from him what he had denied the boy.

"A child is going into the ground today," he yelled at his reflection. "I killed that boy."

"An accident," Ellie said, clamping her arms around him. "People die in accidents every day." She leaned back from him and shook her head. "So, enough, Gavin. Stop. Okay?"

No. It wasn't okay. It was a million miles away from okay.

Two days ago, just after seven in the morning, the boy passed away. *Passed away,* he thought. *Euphemisms. The boy was dead. He ended.*

Even as Ellie helped him into his dark blue suit, he knew he would never wear it again.

Walking without crutches was still painful. He welcomed the pain. The dazzling sunlight pounced on him through the open front door. The weather had turned around. The air hummed with shifting scents, the exaggerated smells stirred by sunshine after rainfall. Bird song, liquid and trilling, crowded the day. There seemed to be smiles inserted into the birds' whistling.

"Gavin, please," Ellie said, easing him towards the car. "You have to do this. You know you do."

He allowed her to take the burden of some of his heaviness. Was he getting fat?

"No, no," he said, crunching over the gravel with her. "I just felt a tad dizzy is all."

When he managed, with Ellie's help, to get into the passenger seat, Ellie returned to the house for his crutches. "Just in case."

Enervated, he was trying to deny the nauseating sensation bubbling in his stomach, when a small boy and his mum passed the front gate. The happy-looking young mother in torn denims leaned down to listen to something the boy, who wore red-framed glasses, wanted to say into her ear. She laughed and swiped a kiss across his cheek. He pulled her back down before she straightened up and pressed his mouth to his mum's face. She picked him up and walked away, clutching the boy in her arms.

Gavin had never witnessed anything so terrifying.

Ellie returned with the crutches and got in the car.

"It's exactly seven days," he said, after a few kilometres.

"Gavin, not now. Please."

"This is important. Hear me on this. Look. The boy was seven. The thing happened today last week. He died at seven o'clock and, well, it must be significant, right?"

They were driving through a busy country town, and, without replying to him, Ellie swerved the car off the main road. The car bumped onto the pavement and Gavin felt a few jolts rattle his ribs. Ellie cursed. Normally she seldom cursed. She closed the windows and flicked on the air-conditioning.

"Sorry," Gavin said. He attempted to twist around to pick one of the crutches off the floor and put it back in the rear seat, but couldn't.

"What?" she asked, trembling now as if she'd emerged from an icy lake, and despite the suffocating heat in the car.

"Sorry," he repeated.

"That's the first time you've apologised since this thing began."

"When I made it to the boy lying on the road, he said 'sorry'. I mean he, the boy I'd ploughed into. He told me he was sorry."

"Why are you doing this?"

"And that's what I said when the police arrived, while we were waiting for the ambulance. I walked up to one of them on the radio, he was. I said, 'I'm sorry, guard'. Only I handed him half of the boy's skateboard. I couldn't find the other part."

"Stop it. Stop it. Stop!" Ellie screamed, with her hands fastened to her ears.

"Sorry."

"And stop saying 'sorry'." She turned on the engine and trundled into the traffic and speeded towards a junction.

"Christ Ellie, be careful," he said, when they were through. "The lights were red. Are you crazy?"

"Okay," she said, wiping the corners of her eyes using the back of her hand. "Let's both try and hold this together." She shot him a glance, and then fixed her hair in the rear-view mirror.

Gavin worked his shaking hands beneath his thighs. "What you said before?" He used conversation as an excuse to study her face. She looked confused. "You said that the boy's parents were holy?"

She smiled and seemed to hold the smile, as though she were practising how to appear happy. "We prayed together in the hospital. The man made a cross here with his fingers." Ellie reached sideways to make the sign of the cross on Gavin's forehead.

He jerked away from her. "Ellie, the road. Look it. That was the church. I think you missed the turn."

A strange cry came from Ellie, a sound that Gavin experienced as a wave breaking inside his stomach. "Hey, come on. It's alright. Just pull in when you can. I'll twist it around."

Gavin felt encased in something like a shroud of relief when Ellie effected a U-turn and insisted that he avoid the driver's seat, at least until after the funeral.

During the funeral mass, Ellie held onto Gavin's hand and arm as though he were a prayer. Gavin wanted to tell her what he was thinking. He would tell her later how he now realised that it was the dog's fault. If the dog hadn't taken the sausages and rashers from the shopping bag on the kitchen floor, he wouldn't have had to go back to Tesco's. And if he hadn't returned to the store, he'd never have seen the advert on the notice board for the golf clubs, and wouldn't have called the number.

There was no reason why he should have been driving in that neighbourhood if it hadn't been for those stupid golf clubs. He wondered whose destiny it was, his or the boy's? Could be that maybe another car might have hit the boy, who skated down the steps and onto the road.

Waiting outside the church somebody said the parents had already left for the cemetery.

They got into the car and followed the cortege out of the town until they arrived at a small graveyard. They stood at the back of the solemn crowd. The priest's words – a faraway mumble.

"I'm sorry," Gavin said when he took the mother's hand after the graveside ceremony. There, he'd done it again. The word sounded vacuous, the helpless cry made by a man in a drowning sea. The boy's mother clasped his hand in both her hands.

"Peter is our only child," she said, making it sound as though he were still alive. "He's a beautiful boy. A special gift to us at our age." Her eyes jumped sideways to a tall middle-aged man next to her.

"I'm Ted," the man said, extending his hand and creasing his large stature at the waist to shake Gavin's hand. "I'm Peter's father."

"I'm so very sorry, sir," Gavin said to the man whose eyes were bursting with accusatory forgiveness.

"The Lord forgives you," the boy's father answered. He smiled a warm smile that would never leave Gavin alone.

"Yes," the boy's mother said. "Thank you both for coming." She took Ellie's black-lace gloved hand. "You know, the day will come when we'll all grow old, and, when that day comes, we must depend upon the love of those around us to carry us towards the next journey. But Peter will remain the boy he was when his father and I said goodbye to him on that blessed night."

They watched the boy's parents receive the offered commiserations of the dispersing crowd with the same graceful acceptance. Gavin allowed Ellie to lead him by the hand towards the car park. At the car she passed him the keys without speaking. She got into the passenger seat and stared straight ahead. She seemed to forget that he needed help climbing into the car.

On the drive home, Gavin said, "That's the only funeral I've ever attended where it didn't rain."

Ellie squirmed in the seat next to him and mumbled. She was sleeping.

He cast his eyes skyward through the windscreen. He could make out a few seagulls at a great height. The sky was an inverted bay, and the gulls gliding around it matched the mastery of fish swimming in water.

Now there has to be something in that, he thought.

In Fields of Butterfly Flames

A St. Bernard pup, my instant pal, he bounded straight to me from the litter of four and the mama dog when I went to collect him. Hardly weaned that evening I brought him home, he didn't last long. Two days later I came in from working the fields to find his little bedraggled body floating in the rusty barrel drum. On the ground beside the barrel, a garden rake with congealed blood and white dog hairs clinging to its steel teeth.

The instant thrumming that started up in my head gave way to petrified anger as I pressed his sopping and lifeless carcass to my face. The heightened doggy smell pervaded my senses and the freezing wetness soaked through my overalls, chilling me beyond chillness. And there I knelt, shivering and snivelling next to the unused outhouse until the September evening closed in, my little pal's remains in my arms, the uneven, stony earth biting into my knees.

The moon threw a bony light across the land. The same ghostly luminosity I remembered playing with the elongated shadows a year before. That terrible night Dale never came home. In the pre-dawn light I found him – what was left of our second born – our only surviving son.

Numbed and helpless, I pushed to my feet and headed for the house, in my arms the St Bernard puppy I hadn't yet named.

Shona was where I knew she'd be, at the kitchen table. Spread before her like tarot cards, family photos taken from the albums featuring Dale, many of them with sides sheared into curved contours where she'd long ago cut out the images of Robert, our eldest, cancelling him as though he, Robert, had never been. As if, by denying Robert's life, she could erase what he'd done to our family and our family home.

In the photos Dale as an infant; Dale's first steps; Dale red-faced pedalling a tricycle on his third birthday, Dale sitting atop the grey Shetland colt; Dale at the seaside; his first Communion, his Confirmation; Dale through a smile that wasn't a smile blowing out eighteen candles on a birthday cake; his nineteenth and twentieth birthdays. And in Shona's hand, as usual, the photo of a cake featuring a Batman motif and the number twenty-one – the birthday Shona had insisted we celebrate in Dale's absence.

With the dead pup cradled in my arms, I waited for Shona to release the photo her thumbs caressed. She didn't. I clenched tight my eyes and shook my head in a futile effort to shake away the images that wouldn't leave me alone: Shona bundling the St. Bernard pup into the barrel. Her maddened, contorted features as she used the garden rake to batter and plunge the screaming and terrified animal beneath the drowning waters.

With bile rising into my throat, I turned from her and for the living room.

In the living room I placed the pup's body on the rug before the hearth, scrunched up some old newspapers and got a fire going to dry out his coat before burial in the morning.

Over the next few weeks, for the best part, I avoided Shona. Did only the necessary jobs to be done with the cattle in the fields and the milking parlour; freeing me with the time I needed to devote to a special project.

The evening I'd been working towards arrived. Only a month since the pup's drowning, and not fully a year since Dale went away, my gut told me Shona still needed way more time. I guessed it'd be this way. That's why I'd spent the last few weeks getting the outhouse ready for the new arrival: put in aluminium window frames with dark, frosted glass and inside shutters, took care of all those areas where draughts might sneak in, and I got hold of a big wicker basket with blankets where he could sleep. The inside walls I replastered, put in a toilet and sink, rewired the electricity, warmed the drying plaster with a small heater and stuck in a small cooker and a mini fridge. The old sofa I'd kept stored in the barn would do me.

The renovated outhouse would also give me a place to escape from Shona – lately she'd been depressing me like I never thought possible. Far more cosy in the house naturally, but my new pal and me would do fine out there. And as for Shona coming mooching around the outhouse, I wasn't concerned. She seldom left the house anymore.

Because my new pal would be quite young, my plan was to stay with him nights, right up until I felt Shona was ready to accept him in the house. No way I would have left him on his own on that cold stone floor beneath those rafters. Not at night-time.

Shona wouldn't be bothered by my absence. Truth is, we hadn't slept in the same bed these past months.

Anyway, I could hardly contain my excitement that first evening. Finally, there he was safe in his basket where I left him. Just how I imagined it. I'd picked him up early that morning. Drove over a hundred miles to get him. He wailed and whimpered for hours for his mama. That was the toughest part of it. He refused to take food and drink, his eyes retreated from mine whenever I got too close, and his body froze like a lamb with hypothermia.

I left a bowl of milk near his basket, and in another bowl some of the reheated rabbit stew I'd cooked up especially the night before. He'd come round. As I said, he was young yet.

I was right. Although, after three or four days, I'd been starting to doubt my convictions, and came very close to bundling him back into the Pajero, driving back to where I picked him up and depositing him in the street. But one day when I came in from the fields at lunchtime, he toppled out of his basket and padded right up to me.

"Hey," I said. "Hello. There's a good boy. You ready to be my friend now?"

He nodded up at me, a tiny even-toothed smile on his face. "Yeah," he said, and jerked up his arms, like a game he was maybe used to playing. "Yeah," he repeated.

"Okay," I said, and playfully copied his arm movements. I then ruffled his curly head, his hair the same russet-red as Dale's, except Dale's had been straight. One of the reasons I'd chosen him: his hair.

Just like the boys when they were kids, my little pal was temperamental. One moment he was giggling and turning the potato chips on his plate into impromptu cars and planes and making engine noises, the next he was blubbering for his mama again. But as soon as I told him we were going to drive the tractor around the fields, he forgot all about his mama. He even put on some of the clothes I'd left out for him. Dale's clothes: striped trousers, a Batman T-shirt, and a pair of blue wellies, stuff that Shona'd kept for a million years. She's a hoarder, Shona. Holds onto everything.

Sitting upfront in the tractor cabin, he could have been one of the boys. He pointed at the screaming seagulls the way the boys used to, and giggled at the blades churning up the earth and his hair smelt just the way theirs did, of shampoo and vitality.

The only time he got a bit confused was when I called him 'Dale'. He stuck out his lower lip, cried, and told me his real name. I eased down on the brakes, killed the engine, and explained that we were playing a pretend game. He could pretend I was his daddy, couldn't he? And I could pretend his name was Dale.

"You're not my daddy," he said, his back pressed to the

tractor door, his features a knot of confusion and fear, the way he appeared the day he arrived.

"No, of course I'm not." I ruffled his untidy hair. "How about 'Pa'? Why don't you call me Pa?"

He made no answer, but his crying stopped. He twisted round, his face and palms pressed against the glass.

"Look," he said, pointing at the darkening sky. "A nail."

Puzzled at first by what he meant, I got it when he glanced and giggled a gurgly giggle at his own wiggling thumb. A fingernail. He saw the quarter moon set in the charcoal-blue sky as a fingernail clipping. What a clever kid. He and Dale really might have been the same boy. Despite being two years younger, Dale was way smarter than Robert. Always was.

For my little pal and me the following weeks fell into a routine, a routine I wished could've lasted forever: once I'd milked the cows, put them out to graze in the low fields, weather permitting, and fed and watered the bay mare, I'd return to Dale – the newest Dale – who'd already be up, sleepy-eyed and waiting, prepare his Coco Pops and juice, get him cleaned up, and then out to the fields, the two of us, where we'd talk, laugh and sing our way through the morning and into the evening in the tractor cabin or mucking about in the fields.

Soon, with the limited daylight, the crops on a go-slow, and Halloween drawing in, there was less reason for us to be out in the fields. Just as well. I was worried about the effects the drop in temperature might be having on the lad. This concern turned into obsession. The old two-bar electric heater and small blow heater hardly made a difference in our converted outhouse: our home. So I pulled out, from a load of junk in the cowshed, a baseboard heater I'd long ago forgotten about.

But despite the three heaters turned up full, the place

never reached room temperature. Must have been the stone floor and the original dampness. So when little Dale began coughing this nasty cough that sounded like he might tear his throat, I knew the time had come. Time to introduce him to Shona.

Completely hidden by the band of conifers, I could make out Shona's familiar seated figure in the square of light at the kitchen table when I emerged along the dirt path clutching Dale's hand. Not knowing for sure how Shona might react when she saw the boy, I warned him that the lady we were going to visit wasn't well. She cried a lot, I told him. Sometimes she screamed. And her eyes were big, like an owl's eyes. But there was no need for him to be afraid. After all, I was with him. I'd never let anything happen to him. His pa would protect him.

"Shona," I said, after I wiped my feet across the worn straw doormat. "I've got a surprise for you."

Just as I'd foreseen, Shona initially ignored me. Her maddened eyes kept right on scouring the photos before her, as if she might yet detect the missing minutiae to undo the unanswerable.

"Son," I said, directing the boy in front of me by the shoulders. "This is your… this is Shona."

In my palms I felt his resistance like the first strike of a brown trout. That sense of being hyper connected to another living creature, its pulse firing along the fishing line and coursing through you, so that you and it are indistinguishable: two beings, one soul.

I smiled reassuringly down at his upturned face, his mouth shaping the word 'Pa' – I was almost sure of it.

The terrible sound that pealed from Shona then was the same scream I'd last heard the morning I came through the open kitchen door, Dale's lifeless body draped across my shoulders in a fireman's lift, and branded around his neck the hanging mark left by the blue rope I sometimes used as a makeshift halter for the bay mare.

"You're frightening him, Shona. Please."

Wedged between the counter, where she now stood, and the accidentally overturned kitchen table, she shook her head, her swollen eyes the predatory eyes of a cornered beast.

Dale had turned away from her, his whole face clenched, his arms about my leg. I picked him up.

"Pa," he said. "Pa."

About to escape clutching the boy, Shona's frozen face shifted, her attention on the scattered photos lying in the black and white tiled floor. A new terror played in her features. And then she was on her knees, scratching at the photos' corners, gathering them together. But what happened next I could never have foreseen.

Dale indicated he wanted to be put down. He then tottered to Shona, crouched next to her and began to scoop up some of the photos. Shona jerked from him, her head sideways, her eyes jammed in their corners.

My entire being coiled, primed to intervene, as I watched Shona's eyes, bubbles in a spirit level, right themselves slowly as she twisted her face towards Dale. The smile that curled her lips retransforming, returning the once beautiful face that, till then, taunted like a memory of something that never was.

"Who's this?" she asked, her gaze locked to Dale the way a lioness locks onto a grazing gazelle from behind tall grass. "Where did you get him?"

"He needs us to look after him," I said. Too soon to even consider using his name on front of Shona. Later. That would come later.

"He's beautiful," she said.

On her knees she opened her arms. Dale hesitated.

Twisted round to me. Sweating, I nodded. And, as in a rare vignette, one that doesn't terrify, dreamed as if under heavy fever, it happened. Dale kind of stumbled forward and fell into Shona's motherly embrace.

"There, there," she said. "Mo chuisle. Mo chuisle mo chroi," using the language of her rural background. *My pulse. My pulse of my heart.*

From that moment, Shona and Dale were as inseparable and steadfast as a successful peach and pear tree grafting.

In the mornings shafts of autumn sunlight through the kitchen window animated their lively togetherness. Dale sang nursery rhymes with Shona, his piping voice blending with the warbling and trilling that poured in from the hazel trees and yew hedging in the garden. Evening times they sat together at the kitchen table making fairy cakes and gingerbread men. And from a book I hadn't seen for years, Shona read to him tales of ants and eagles, wolves and lions, foxes and crows. Dale's eyes swelled bigger than a puppy's, his laughing voice pre-empting words spoken by fabled creatures whose lives he already knew and relived during Shona's reading.

All seemed renewed. Like the imminent catastrophes magically overridden in those fantastic fables, beauty and harmony to the world had been restored. And yet inside my stomach there bubbled something evil, a warning that wouldn't leave me alone. And I, in turn, refused the temptation to leave Dale alone with Shona. Perhaps because she insisted Dale call her by her name. While she only ever addressed Dale as 'love' or 'a stor mo chroi' – *treasure of my heart.*

Could be that I imagined it, but there was another thing: in Shona's eyes an occasional glint that reminded me of certain dogs I've owned or encountered over the years. A wild look, an emptiness that cancelled every trace of thousands of years' domesticity would sizzle in their canine eyes. The eye glint that flashed before the attack, the sudden, unexpected snap and snarl when teeth connected with outstretched hand.

Never would I allow her to be alone with him, I vowed. Not ever.

The dairy herd lowing in the barn to be milked in the early mornings I tried to ignore. Not until Dale was up and finished his breakfast did I leave the house, with Dale in my arms or tottering sleepily beside me. The big basket from the outhouse I'd removed and placed in the milking parlour. While I got the milking machine going and hooked up the teat cups, Dale curled up under his blankets, asked endless questions, sang snatches of nursery rhymes and usually fell asleep.

Shona's endless pleading it was that altered this routine.

"A little mite," she kept at me. "And you dragging him out into the cold. Is it mad you are?"

"Good for the lad," I said. "It'll toughen him up. Turn him into a hardy soul."

But Shona wouldn't leave off her badgering. And she seemed to be deteriorating again. The signs were obvious. Even pulled out the photo album one afternoon.

Finally, I relented. No choice. But not before I'd reexplained to Dale that Shona wasn't well. And that sometimes adults who are unwell do things they don't mean to. Like hurt people. I gave him a spare key to the outhouse, showed him how to use it and how to lock himself inside should he ever feel that Shona was going to hurt him. There he was to stay till I came to get him.

"Do you understand? You come here and lock yourself in like this, and I'll be here soon. Okay?"

He got it. I could tell. Such a bright kid.

Unconvinced, however, about Shona's mental state, I

hurried in from the parlour with beating temples and knotted stomach at what horror scene awaited me that first day I left him alone with her. And this pattern I continued at half-hourly intervals throughout the day and days that followed during the week. My dinner during that period I could hardly look at.

But just when the beating in my head began to ease, and a healthy appetite usurped my twisted stomach, I emerged from the conifer grove one evening to a sight that caught me in the solar plexus. Hot, bitter bile erupted from my throat and spilled through my lips. Enervated, I drew my sleeve across my mouth and squinted towards the house.

In the kitchen window a shimmering orange light centred on the ledge replaced the normal light: the pumpkin they'd been carving that afternoon. Absent were Dale and Shona's figures.

Into an impulsive sprint I broke and reached the house in seconds.

"Dale!" I shouted, as I pounded through the house. "Shona. Dale," I heard my detached voice bellowing, while I pulled open doors, crashed into furniture and fittings and tore away crumpled bedclothes.

Gone – both of them. What had she done? What had I let that fiend do?

In my urgency to get back down the stairs, I slipped. Something detonated inside my ankle, sending a metallic sheet of pain exploding across my vision. Working my way back onto my feet at the bottom of the stairs, a follow-up explosion, raw and crimson, erupted behind my eyes, buckling me like a shot hind. Pushing through the blinding pain, I dragged myself over the floor and to the kitchen. There I summoned greater willpower and strength than I could have imagined I possessed, and pressed, pulled and pushed my way on one leg.

Using the sweeping brush as a crutch, I tried to steel myself against the inevitable horror forming in my head. The barrel drum. I had to get to the barrel drum.

Every movement down the three steps from the kitchen into the yard brought intolerable sledgehammer blows slamming against my ankle. I clenched my teeth and released intermittent growls: ugly, guttural sounds, the snarls of a creature in deep distress, or a murderer, maybe.

Too far from the shimmering light in the kitchen window, I could just about make out the pallet that acted as a makeshift lid removed and resting against the barrel's side.

Fractured images of the drowned pup changed to Dale's stiffened body hanging from the outhouse rafters, and of Robert, almost two years before him, on the floor of that same outhouse, his head half-blown away, my Magnum hunting rifle next to him, bleeding his life away in my lap. The images splashed about amongst the swirling pain.

The barrel, half-hidden by the shade thrown beneath the eaves of the low-pitched roof, made it impossible to see inside the container. So I plunged my arm through the blackened water up to my shoulder. The Arctic coldness cutting into my flesh, right through to the bone marrow, gave instant respite from the intolerable burning flailing of my ankle.

Empty. The barrel was empty.

Relieved, confused, terrified, I snapped my head backwards at the night sky and cursed the nothingness. The sickening pain shooting from my ankle to my head I welcomed.

Robert and Dale dead. Somehow, as their father, their deaths belonged to me. And now, I had surely killed Dale again.

More than pain, I too deserved death. But before I

accepted and administered the self-inflicted punishment, I had to behold Dale's twisted and slain form. My instincts pushed me on through the yard towards the outhouse.

Unaccustomed to strange movements once they'd been housed for the night, the cattle hoofed about uneasily in the barn, grunting and complaining. The bay mare, from her stable, whinnied and blew for my attention. I limped onward towards the outhouse.

Drawing near I thought I could see a sliver of light slicing through the window shutter. I pushed on harder.

Scrabbling in my overalls for the keys when I reached the door, I could swear I heard a voice or voices whispering inside. I stopped. I listened... Yes. Shona's voice and, Jesus, it couldn't be... could it? I eased down the door handle and peered through the gap.

Silence now. Then from behind the door...

"Boo." Dale.

I fell backwards, renewed pain lacerating my ankle. But I didn't care.

"Dale," I said. "Dale. You're... You're okay."

"Pa fall down, Shona," he said twisting round to her. "Pa fall down." And he came to me, his little hands gripping my arm, his face fully concerned, in a huge effort to drag me to my feet.

"Oh my God," Shona said, stepping into the night. "Are you okay?"

Shona's immediate suggestion that she call an ambulance I countered.

"No, Shona. "I'll be fine. Really. It's just a sprain. Ice. You guys help me inside and, eh, ice. From the mini fridge. Ice." Ensuring Shona was fully focused my way, I allowed my eyes to jump in Dale's direction. I raised my eyebrows and nodded. A look I hope she'd get.

Her eyes, alighting on Dale, narrowed. She pursed her

lips. She got it. Neither one of us needed the authorities sniffing around the farm.

Once they helped me inside, and Shona made up an ice pack, placed a mug of tea before me and explained how Dale had brought her by the hand to what he called 'the uddy house', she and Dale sat down together at the table and got on with what they'd clearly been doing before I arrived.

"Look," she said to Dale. "I found another one that fits."

Dale clapped his hands and giggled.

Sticking the cut up photos back together. Christ. She'd kept the images of Robert. She never could discard anything.

"Oh look," she said. "There you are with Robert, Dale. The day we had the picnic by the lake. The day it snowed in March."

Another explosion rocketed skyward in my head. But this time a fireworks explosion crowded with an unbearable feeling of pure joy. But as the coloured trails and sparks burned away, they took with them my fleeting elation. Deposited in its place despair – instant, utter and complete.

Robert. Robert and Dale. Dale and Robert. Never were two lads more inseparable than our boys. Two years between them, they were best buddies from the day we brought Dale home from the hospital. So close were they, Dale stuck right by his big brother when Robert got sick, when Robert's head betrayed him, made him think crazy thoughts and do terrible things.

Like that summer, Robert's last summer, when he trapped butterflies. Convinced the butterfly swarms were descending on the farm as a locust plague. He started out by pinning the insects to the old picnic table by the lake with bramble bush thorns. He'd then place a magnifying glass between them and the sun, his eyes widening, and his nostrils expanding, as he pulled in the wispy smoke plumes rising from the smouldering carcases.

A failure on my part to get the boy help, I admit it. He graduated to trapping butterflies in the hundreds. That's all he did that summer. Trapped them and kept them in an old reptile cage he had in his bedroom. Sometimes he'd set them free in the room and just sit in his computer chair, this look on his face, watching the butterflies flit about, alighting on bookshelves and picture-frames, or thrashing against the window for freedom.

Afraid of the consequences I was. Shona too. We discussed it. We'd work through his troubles as a family.

Too late. I got a call one afternoon from the emergency services to get back quickly to the farm. Shona, Dale and I were at the weekend market operating the vegetable stall. There'd been an accident, the guy on the phone warned.

The flames were still devouring the farmhouse when I pulled up outside the gate to our home: patrol cars, fire brigades and flashing lights. They'd cordoned off the entrance, the police or the firemen. Neighbours had gathered.

"Robert," I shouted at the policemen trying to restrain me from pushing past the bodies and the vehicles. "My son Robert is inside. Please, I have to…"

"He's safe," the sergeant said, his hands on my shoulders. "We have him. He's safe. It's okay." For his own safety, he told me, they had him in one of the cars. He pointed.

I pushed past.

"Excuse me," I said. "My son. Can you let me through, please?" The crowd made way.

"Robert," I said, tugging open the car door. "Robert, are you okay? What happened?"

But Robert was already somewhere else. Wasn't even

aware of my presence. His bloated face, crammed with concentration, never shifted from the inferno, the flames flickering in his pupils and dancing on his skin. From his throat a sickening, high-pitched keening caused the guard seated next to him to snap the cuffs attached to their wrists.

"Relax," the young guard said. "Take it easy now."

I frowned at the handcuffs and then at the guard.

"For his own safety," the guard replied. "For his own safety, sir."

And for Robert's safety, and ours, we finally had him committed for a while, but he talked us into getting the doctor to sign his release. The provision being that he continued to take the prescribed drugs.

Robert fooled us there too.

Twenty-three months. Dale waited twenty-three months before he followed Robert. We failed to read the signs. All summer he'd been talking about how, his next birthday, he'd be exactly the age Robert was when his brother went away. Dale just couldn't cope without him.

Tomorrow. Tomorrow was Halloween. I'd get Shona to drive into town for a Batman outfit. Then, in the evening, we could all head off like a family in Shona's car to some other town – a faraway town, where nobody knew us. Shona would understand. Crowded with compassion now, she was ready to forgive. While I sat in the car with my bandaged ankle, she and Dale could go trick-or-treating. The perfect day and time to seek out Dale's big brother Robert, lost and lonely out there somewhere, waiting. Waiting for forgiveness.

Too Damn Beautiful

But Friday nights were pizza nights. As soon as the kids were gone to bed, they would order in and watch a movie. That was the rule. And it was her turn to choose from Netflix. He put his hands on her waist, looked into her eyes, and agreed that yes, of course it was. But the thing is, see, he'd had pizza at lunchtime. One of the girls in the office was leaving and they surprised her with a going-away lunch.

"I've already got *Titanic* lined up," she said. She stamped her foot on the carpet like a child. "I've been looking forward to it the whole week."

"Come on, Rach," he said. "It's just this one time." The rugby semi-final was on. Between Leinster and Scarlets.

"It's not fair." She whacked away his hands from off her hips. She folded her arms. "And another thing. You didn't tidy up last night. Or put the plates in the dishwasher. It was your turn."

"I'm sorry, baby. It's been a mad week. With all the extra bullshit I have to do these days." He reached out a hand towards her face.

She jerked from him. "Don't touch me, David." She spat his name like a curse.

"Come on, baby, please."

Without saying another word, she picked up the red notebook from the coffee table, twisted about and left the room. The door she closed gently.

"Bastard," she said, in the hall. More about him than at him. Though over the raised up sound of the pre-match sports panel he wouldn't have heard her anyway.

While she crept up the stairs, she could hear the girls, *his girls*, giggling and whispering. And she heard too the click of the light switch. And then silence. Looking in on them would only give them the excuse to start up again. She passed their bedroom door and went into her own room, careful not to wake the baby. *Her baby.*

She resisted the temptation to wake him, so she could put him in the bed beside her. Instead she switched on the bedside lamp and lay down on top of the duvet. She then opened the red notebook and went through this week's list. Apart from Monday, she'd prepared breakfast every day, although he had put the lunches together for the girls. And sure why wouldn't he? Why shouldn't he? They were his girls.

She was aware of her own increased breathing through her nostrils as she went through the itemised chores. He'd done the shopping on Wednesday, but she had prepared the grocery list. The laundry, including his dirty underwear, she had picked up off chairs and off the floor and put into the washing machine. And, of course, she was the one to empty it and put the clothes in the drier. This week it was supposed to have been his job. He was rostered. She put ticks beside what he had done and crosses next to what he was supposed to do but hadn't.

When she was through with checking the list, she considered storming back downstairs and presenting him with her findings. She decided against it. Unlike their friends' marriages, theirs was going to work. They too, she and he, had had separate failed marriages. For six years she lived with someone she never really knew. Not until she got pregnant did he decide to take himself off one weekend when she was visiting her sister in London. A text message. That's all the bastard could manage. A fucking text message to say he was '*moving on*'. And David's wife had taken her own life. Left a note saying she just couldn't cope anymore. When David spoke about her to Rachel, his voice always grew angry. "Cope?" he'd say, frowning at Rachel as if it were she who had written the note and taken an overdose. "Cope? And did she ever think about how I'm supposed to cope with two young girls to bring up on my own?"

Rachel and David had met each other through an online dating agency. Neither of them had lied too much in their personal profiles. He described himself as 'an almost young, widowed father of two girls', which made Rachel smile. And she, in turn, went so far as to include a picture of herself with her baby. When they first met, he greeted her with two kisses. Very continental, she thought, which clinched it for her. While, for him, as he told her often, the moment he saw her smile, he knew that he would spend the rest of his life waking up to that pretty face.

The roster outlining their shared domestic duties they had put together methodically as a way of avoiding a second marital breakdown for each of them. She claimed it was her idea, he said it was his. Finally, they agreed that they had both come up with it together.

Whosoever idea it was, the core purpose was that by dividing the indoor and outdoor chores fairly, they could avoid the inevitable tension that arises in a relationship when one side does more work than the other.

Rachel, who had read an online article recently on the power of positivity, decided she would put the time not watching TV to good use. She opened up the new book she'd bought for their forthcoming holiday to Tenerife. She read the first page and turned to the second, only to realise she had taken nothing in. She returned to the opening, but stopped to check her Smartphone. Just some junk emails. Tempted to log on to Facebook, she recalled another online article that claimed people were becoming more stupid thanks to technology and our addiction to social networking sites. She began the first chapter again, but something else niggled at her. The book's title: *Go Set a Watchman.* What was that supposed to mean? She lay the book on his pillow, cover up, and checked its meaning on Wikipedia. There were references to the Bible, and Isaiah, whoever he was?

She clutched her phone to her chest and closed her eyes. She thought about their holiday to Tenerife. This would be their first trip together as a family. The images of golden beaches, azure blue bays and suntanned bodies gave her a pleasant feeling in her stomach. She saw herself applying suncream to the girls' bodies. Playing her role as stepmum. And there would be handsome waiters to serve them, other people to prepare their meals, no need to worry about whose turn it was to do the cleaning. No reluctant trips to the supermarket. A break from the arguments about the school run.

The next thing Rachel was aware of was the sound of David in the bathroom. She'd fallen asleep. She reached out for her book and knocked it off the bed. She left it where it fell. From the bathroom she could hear him making hawking noises. Something she hated. She threw her feet over the side of the bed, stood up and slipped off her skirt and top. And just before he was in the room, she got herself back in the bed and under the duvet.

"Hey, baby," he said.

With her back to him, she stayed quiet.

"Are you asleep?"

She listened to him hurriedly shucking off his clothes. She knew what that meant. The cold air pawed at her when he lifted the duvet. Already at the edge of her side of the mattress, she brought her arm out from under the duvet and laid it flat upon the bed, marking the boundary between them. And she tucked the middle of the duvet under her body.

He tried to push close to her.

“No,” she said.

“Ah, c’mon, Rach, don’t be like that.” He tried to palm her ass.

She tensed her entire body. “I mean it. Keep your hands off me.”

He made a sucking sound with his tongue off the roof of his mouth, and twisted from her, his back to hers. “Okay.”

That was that. She could relax. If there was one thing about his character that was unbending, it had to be his pride. Something Rachel always admired in him. And with this reawakened feeling for him came a sense of pity. She was denying him the one thing that always brought them as close as any two people can ever come. Some of the things he said to her during those moments of intimacy almost undermined her willpower. The way he looked, not into her eyes but, into her soul, his contorted expression so cute, and told her how he wished they could stay that way forever. And then there were the words she never tired of hearing, when he told her how damn beautiful she was. Or how, not until he met her, did he realise that there had to be a God.

Soon, David was snoring next to her. Unable to return to sleep, she began in her head a new list. A list of all the things about him that she loved and those she didn’t. She began with the positives. Top of the list was his insistence always in jumping out of the car and running around to her side and opening her door. And she loved too the way he had of looking from each of her eyes to the other. And his appearance. Okay, so he wasn’t George Clooney, although they shared the same age, but he had a rugged handsomeness. Those smile lines about his eyes. Something her friends generally agreed about. She continued with the list till she reached ten things.

The second part of the list came much more quickly,

beginning with what she had realised very soon into their relationship was an innate selfishness. At first, she joked about this, using one of her dad's quips. His three favourite people she told him were me, myself and I. And then there was the way he sometimes paid more attention to people around them in public than to her. And of course the comments he made, always too loud, about others, usually couples. What the hell did she see in that guy? Or, your man had to have money. How could anybody let themselves go like that?

When she reached number ten on the second part of the list, she stopped. She could have gone on but didn't.

Accentuate the positive. Another of her dad's wisdoms. Perhaps she'd been unreasonable. David's job had become more demanding lately. Too much administration. If she thought about it before, she could understand why he hadn't been attending properly to his chores about the house. At bottom, David was a good man, a loving husband, and a caring father. To her baby as much as the girls. The way to salvage their marriage came to her the way things sometimes did. In an instant. Through what she believed as divine intervention. But she suspected more through her dead father.

Rachel loosened the duvet and shifted into the centre of the bed, her back to him. She pressed into his manly warmth. He mumbled. She slipped free from her bra, took his hand and cupped it over her left breast.

The next morning, she got up early. Hours before the children's channels came on air. She fixed some coffee and took it and herself into what they called the computer room and logged on. She was on a mission.

The fruits of that mission, a Nigerian girl called Chantel, arrived for duty on Tuesday afternoon. Rachel's day off. The girl was about Rachel's height, but far slimmer. She wore tight grey leggings and a dark top. On her face she wore a permanent smile. Rachel had never seen such perfect white teeth. She supervised the girl for the first hour, ensuring she knew exactly what she had to clean and attend to and how Rachel wanted it done. She left her alone for the second hour, while Rachel went to pick up the kids from school.

When she returned home with the girls, David's Jeep was parked in the driveway. Inside she was surprised to find the girl still there. She and David were sitting at the kitchen table drinking tea.

"Hi Rach," he said. He told her he'd knocked off early to make up for Friday. Thought they'd all go out for a pizza.

"Yay, pizza. Pizza," the girls said.

Rachel replied she didn't feel up to it, but that he and the kids should go ahead. She'd stay home with the baby.

The housekeeping girl walked out with David and the girls. And, if she wasn't imagining it, Rachel saw his hand slip down from the small of her back and tap her lightly on the ass. David turned around to say he was running Chantel down to the bus stop. Something they seemed to have already arranged.

Thursday afternoon, David's day to do the school run, Chantel arrived, as agreed, for housekeeping duties.

On Friday evening, David sent Rachel a text letting her know he was snowed under with paperwork and wouldn't be home till late. While she was trying to call him, a follow up text came in to say he'd done the figures, and that they'd have to forgo the holiday to Tenerife. What with the crèche and now the housekeeping charges, they just couldn't afford a holiday.

Maybe next year.

Forever Chasing Pigeons

The tables were too close together. A light breeze shook the sun umbrella. Something, a leaf or a stalk, spiralled onto the white tablecloth. He flicked it away.

Next to their table was a German couple with a toddler. He watched Shelley, watching the boy.

The boy's hair was blonde like Jamie's hair, except Jamie's had been curly. He had to distract her. He braced himself for a scene.

"Shelley, you shouldn't drink so much -"

"You're pathetic. Waiter," she called, snapping her fingers over his shoulder.

"Shelley. Please."

"Shut up."

The waiter arrived.

"Madam?"

"More wine." She held up her empty glass as though she were proposing a toast.

Making the fleetest of bows, the waiter plucked the wine bottle from the bucket stand next to the table, popped the cork and, clutching the bottle with both hands, refilled her glass. Shelley watched the procedure much as someone might study an alchemist transferring a potion from one vial to another.

With rounded eyes locked to her glass, Shelley emptied the drink through a smile that seemed as empty as this whole charade.

Friends and other non-professional do-gooders, along with marriage guidance councillors and psychologists, had given them the same advice from the start. Go back, they said. The only way to move forward was to return to the source of that which initially undermined their relationship.

So here they were, confronting their fears, resurrecting the past, moving forward.

"The pâté is really good," he said.

Shelley's eyes snapped from their focused gaze on the German boy. "How often do I have to tell you?"

He cast about him. Her tone was far too loud. "Not here, please." He offered the German guy an apologetic smile.

"Who are we to eat?" she asked. "Or do anything else, for that matter, while Jamie is locked up in a cold basement somewhere being…" she paused, "you know what, for two years?"

"Stop. We don't know where he is, okay? You have no right…"

"Don't talk to me about rights. And his name is 'Jamie'. You never use Jamie's name. Jamie. Jamie."

"I'm sorry," he called after the German family who were leaving without finishing their meal.

"You and your uppity friends," she went on, "with their villas in Spain, their yachts in the Mediterranean…"

"Can we stop, please?" he interrupted.

"No, we can't stop. My baby is gone because of you and your camera club and golf, your stupid networking -"

"I'm leaving," he answered, trying to catch the waiter's eye for the cheque.

"Go!" she screamed. "Get out of my life."

Why had he listened to them, all those know-it-alls and do-gooders? They shouldn't have returned.

He gave up on the waiter, the bastard. He dropped his eyes to the mushy remains on his plate: tagliatelle. "People are looking," he whispered.

"Murderer," she said. She hissed the word.

"Don't you ever say that. Never even think it. He's alive. Jamie's alive." There, he'd used Jamie's name. Proven her wrong.

That's when the waiter arrived. He paid the bill with a fifty. He'd nothing smaller. But while he was waiting for his change, Shelley got up and pushed off. He followed her without receiving his change – a handsome tip for the waiter. Shelley had to be watched.

He let her keep ahead of him. The red outfit she wore made it easy to tail her. Though he wished she'd keep to the shadows.

Holding Shelley in his snared vision, he could see, peripherally, through the façade masquerading as gaiety. Laughter, forced and aggressive, rained about his heavy shoulders. Who were they convincing, these people, themselves or others?

Shelley's maddened, speeded-up walk brought them to the large square. The square was much the way it was on the same date two years ago, the twelfth of May. The day they last saw Jamie.

On the surface everything seemed ordered and ordinary. What you'd expect in a large square on a roasting afternoon. Old men sat together three or four to a shaded bench. Their tired eyes stared out from leather-coloured faces, whose expressions seemed to ask why they were yet part of a world in which they no longer played a role.

Ancient-looking women, whose black shawls and clothing were flags displaying their widowed status, huddled together on separate benches to the men. And then there were the young pairings: boys straddling backless benches faced their giggling girlfriends who sat cross-legged, kissing and listening to the boys.

Most poignant of all were the toddlers doing what toddlers do, and what Jamie had been doing on this very date two years ago, chasing pigeons.

If Shelley was finally going to be predictably unpredictable, now was the *when* and this was the *where*.

He worked his way in the direction of the square's centrepiece, a tall obelisk, where Shelley had positioned herself on a patch of lawn below the obelisk's pedestal. At an unbiased glance all seemed ordinary. But beneath the snapshot of urbane, everyday life was a sinister core. From the viewpoint of an amateur photographer, he recalled how their world had turned around forever back on that evil day.

Their first holiday together as a family, he had been keen to try out his new camera equipment.

A fresh flock of pigeons landed at the far end of the square, catching Jamie's attention. Jamie charged towards them, with Shelley behind him. Even better. This gave him a reason to put his telescopic lens into action.

He had almost used up a black and white twenty-six exposure when he became aware that his camera lens was making new discoveries. A shapely, yet somehow manly-looking woman he had earlier noticed being approached by an elderly man was now in full-blown conversation with a respectable seeming guy in a beige suit. Despite her vague manliness, the woman stirred something inside him.

Over six feet tall, wearing a silky red micro skirt that barely covered the tops of her thighs, and a face that belonged to one of the women in the *pay as you view* movie channels on the TV back in the hotel room. He understood why men would want her. He too wanted her.

Lest someone might have seen what he was up to, he allowed his zoom lens to roam freely around the square, sliding across the cobblestones, scampering up the trees and searching the skies before swooping down again upon his subject.

For a woman of her vocation she possessed a rough elegance. He eased down on the button. *Click.* Beautiful. He snapped again. Lovely. He zoomed in on her face before pulling back from the viewfinder. Shelley was returning with Jamie.

He busied himself cleaning the camera lens with a small blue cloth.

Shelley's queasiness had returned, she told him. She'd taken too much sun. He suggested they go back to the hotel.

"I'll be fine," she said. "I just need a glass of water, or a coffee maybe. Jamie is having so much fun." She bent down to Jamie and kissed him, telling him to go back and play with the birdies.

"Birdies," Jamie mimicked. "Birdies. Birdies."

"Keep an eye on him," she said. "I'll be back in a minute."

He remembered timing Shelley. So premeditated. To the café at the far side of the square, it took her almost ninety seconds. During that minute and a half his eyes bounced from Shelley to his watch face to Jamie to the manly-woman dealing with the man in the beige suit.

Near the obelisk, Jamie was concentrating on one particular pigeon, a fine-breasted white bird with black flecking. Already the boy had a good eye, just like his dad.

He swung his camera round on the tripod and focused on the woman. He snapped. The shot was good. She shook her head in a definitive *not interested* manner. *Click.* And then she crossed her long, muscular legs away from the beige-suited man. He caught the image squarely. The shutter speed was precise.

Excitement churned about in his stomach at the developing image in the dark room of his mind. But the final shot, the shot he took when the woman obviously got what she had been holding out for, would be the snap of the day, if not the holiday.

Standing a good head over the average-sized man when she stood up, she bent slightly, hitched up one side of her tiny skirt and adjusted something. Bingo.

He saw exactly what the action signified. That's what made the shot unique.

At the opposite side of the square he had noticed a guy in a white T-shirt leaning against a car. As soon as the woman had hitched up her skirt, the white T-shirt slipped into his car and drove off. The skirt thing was a signal. The guy in the white T-shirt, her boss, had read the signal.

That was the last rational thought he had before everything that ever made any sense drifted into oblivion, a rowing boat far out to sea being dragged into the blackened void on a night that seeped up from hell.

Although lathered in sweat and parched with thirst, an icy chill shot through him at the sound of Shelley's voice.

"Where's Jamie?" she said. "Where is he? Where's my baby?"

Hearing himself calling out Jamie's name, he experienced the detached disorientation of a dream, someone else's dream. He was both watcher and the watched in a nightmare so improbable the dreamer is desensitised to the point that he suspects the dream may be a dream of a dream.

By the time the police arrived, Shelley was accosting strangers, yelling into their faces incoherent pleas to give her back her baby.

And now, two years later, he watched Shelley staring out from the obelisk's shadow.

The small children, whose innocent, piping voices played in accompaniment with birdsong, liquid and trilling, were the object of her disturbed and disturbing fascination.

He sniffed hard, wiped the corners of his eyes with his wrists and drew in a long gulp of oxygen. The searing air slashed his lungs.

Shelley ignored him when he placed himself in front of

her. An oniony stink rose from his own body. "Shelley," he said. "Come on. There's nothing left for us here."

For a moment she seemed to look at him in bewilderment. Her eyes were vacant. No recognition. No emotion. Nothing. He tried again. "We can change the flights, go back home tomorrow. Come on, Shelley. Give me your hand."

"Don't touch me," she said, jerking from his extended arm. "Go away. Leave. Get out of my life forever." A smile that wasn't a smile curled her lips. "Murdering bastard," she added. This last sentiment screeched from her, sending a huge flock of ground-feeding pigeons exploding into the air.

A crowd of people formed round them quickly, yipping and yapping, ravenous for answers. They snuffled at each other hungrily, a pack of curs blooded to a frenzy by a foreign scent.

Shelley's normally ashen complexion, now gorged with blood, was the bright red of her summer dress. And though her mouth appeared as a circular black hole, he couldn't hear the concomitant sound. Hers was a scream that belonged to a face that haunts the dreamer in a fevered sleep.

This frozen image, depicting the silently screaming woman, no longer Shelley, burrowed and burned itself into his consciousness. The corrupted features mocking a pretty face he had once adored, an image that would never leave him alone.

Set next to this still was a picture bursting with happiness and potential.

Morning time: a large square, silver-bordered in a fine mist whooshing from the water sprinklers glistens in the sun. At the centre of this scene is a small boy, a boy who would never have to endure the horrors that came with growing up: a little boy forever chasing pigeons.

The Hanging Tree

Five years old I was when my granny told me bluebottles were ‘dirty things’. So I squished them between the net curtain and the front window. The white mush expelled by the tiny carcases gave off a nasty pungency that tickled the inside of my nostrils. This stink I could avoid by alternatively removing the bluebottles’ wings and sticking pins into the bug bodies.

Then there were the elements. I drowned insects by placing them with a twig standing upright in a bottle, poured water slowly into its nozzle, forcing them to climb higher until there was no dry surface for refuge. Another method was to pinion them to the old wooden garden table with rose thorns, hold a magnifying glass between them and the sun and smell them sizzle. Smothering them was fun, too. Butterflies in a sealed jar went the quickest. Their frantic wingbeats thrashed against the glass, speedily transforming their painted perfection to a pathetic, transparent butterfly skeleton.

By the time I was eight I’d graduated to bigger game like mice and small birds. The other kids in the neighboured, including Decko, my brother, who was two years older than me, were still on their placing frogs on the road and riding over them with the wheels of their bikes-stage.

“You’re only a bunch of chickens,” I said one day when I arrived with a surprise for them in a shoebox.

Aller O’Callaghan, the bully of our country town, made a show of being real mad and slammed his bike to the ground with a clatter.

“What did you call me, you pygmy-midget?” he said, ignoring Decko who was playing along and trying to placate him. Decko held Aller by the other arm.

"He's just a kid, Aller," Decko said. "I'll give you a fight if you want."

"Watch this," I said. I opened the shoebox, grabbed the live brown mouse by its tail and held it up to Aller's face. It would be funny to be able to report that he squealed like a pig, but what that barbecued piece of pork did was scream like a little girl in ankle socks.

Depositing the wriggling mouse on the ground, I whipped the hurley stick from the back of my parked bike and tore after the terrified rodent. It, I told them as soon as I squashed it into the tarmac, at least had a sporting chance, unlike the frogs.

Decko was there to protect me. I knew he would. He convinced Aller that what I did was really cool. Aller listened to Decko. Everyone liked Decko.

Decko was right. He was always right. He was right in the same way the pictures he drew in pencil and charcoal were right. He could've been the best artist ever. I miss him.

Decko thought things out. That's why whenever my friend Ger and me hatched one of our endless plans to make some money, we always brought the idea to Decko first; like the time when we decided to murder Susu O'Gorman. Susu's eyes were big and round and bulged out of his head. His legs were stubby and he had trouble breathing. Susu was one of Mrs. O'Gorman's Pekinese dogs.

The plan was to let her know that Susu was dead, and then send her a threatening note demanding a crisp new tenner or we'd poison the other two dogs.

Mrs. O'Gorman's brain didn't work too well. Older boys called her 'Mad Mary'. But we thought it was funny calling her Mary, her being old enough to be somebody's granny's granny.

"How are you going to poison them?" Decko asked us,

while we were having our secret meeting at the top of Ladders' Tree in the woods behind the church.

"With poison," Ger said, and gave a laugh that was broken into precise syllables.

Ger's eyelashes were longer than anybody's; they always reminded me of that big black bird that was housed all alone in Dublin Zoo: the hornbill. When Ger blinked, his eyelids stayed closed long enough for you to tap him on the shoulder and be looking the other way when he opened them again. It used to take him what seemed like an hour to eat an ice-pop. He took each lick as though he was thinking of nothing, just savouring the tangy orange or sweet vanilla flavour sliding down his throat and dancing on his taste buds.

"Where'll you get the poison?" Decko wanted to know.

"We'll make it," I said, "or rob it."

Decko's eyes creased for a second, and the muscles in his cheeks bunched up. "Don't be stupid. How can you make sure to poison one dog and not the other two?"

Ger and me looked at each other and shrugged our shoulders. Decko went on.

"Even if you succeeded in poisoning one of them, how are you supposed to collect the money? And why do you need 'a crisp new tenner' anyway? Money is money."

Ger and me were trying hard not to look at each other, as the silence had already gone on too long and we knew the other was on the verge of exploding into nervous laughter.

"Got it," he said, and held the knife up as though he were a teacher about to make a point with a cane. "We dognap it."

A cold shudder of delight rippled through my insides, and skeleton fingers crawled around the back of my neck.

"We bring it here and stash it in the old cowshed," he continued. "Then we go back to Mrs. O'Gorman and tell her that a skinhead has her dog and wants ten pounds to give it back."

"The police," Ger said, and slowly blinked.

"Easy," Decko said. "We'll say the skinhead told us to warn her 'No cops', or the dog snuffs it." Decko was crazy about all those detective stories on TV.

We took our intended dognapping very seriously and, with Decko's guidance, planned it in detail over the coming week.

It was July 1974. Older girls were jiggling around in hot pants. That, together with the smell of boiling tar on the roads melting under a hot sun, and Terry Jacks on the radio singing about dying and being no longer a boy, all made me feel so alive, so part of the world that was created just for me, an eleven-year-old boy whose pockets would soon be full of money.

"Bags I be the one to kill Susu if Mrs. O'Gorman brings in the cops," I said later that evening.

The thing is I didn't really want to kill the dog. I just said it to sound like a tough guy. But when Ger and Decko protested that, no, they'd be the ones to destroy the evidence, we convinced each other that we must get the money or the dog was history.

This depressed me and, for a while, I didn't feel as overjoyed as I should've felt about not being Terry Jacks. You see, Mrs. O'Gorman often visited our house. I wasn't sure why she was there, but kind of knew she wasn't one of Mam's friends. When Decko or me, or sometimes Dad, saw her shuffling her way up the front path, or recognised her silhouette through the frosted glass of the front door, we automatically ran into the kitchen to let Mam know, in excited tones, that she was here. There followed a frenzy of whispering panic.

"Jesus," Mam invariably said, "she'll be here all day. Quick, my coat."

"Answer the door, Mam," Decko or me would say. "C'mon."

"I'll tell her I'm on my way out," was Mam's predictable solution.

But she never did carry out her threat to pretend she was just getting ready to leave the house. Mrs. O'Gorman usually ended up exactly as Mam predicted. She sat for hours in the small living room, the room that was soon to become, for Mam, a kind of living tomb.

Even though she had a lot more stripes on her face than my granny, I liked Mrs. O'Gorman. She always reminded me of a nervous little animal, perfectly alert to everything going on around it. Yet there was something weird about her too. She never stopped laughing. And she didn't just laugh for a few seconds like everyone else. She laughed about a million times.

"You look smashing in your brother Declan's T-shirt," she said on one of those visits which seemed weekly, but probably wasn't more than once or twice a month.

"So tell me, how old are you now, Richard?" she continued, still laughing, while scanning the room to probably make a mental inventory of the ornaments and maybe checking the condition of the furniture.

"Eleven-years-old," I said.

"Eleven, is it?" And such a big boy. How old do you think I am?"

"About a hundred," I said.

"One hundred," she shrieked in a tiny voice that sounded as if it were coming from behind a room with a closed door. She threw her head back, shut her eyes for a moment, lifted her miniature legs off the floor, slammed her hands down in her lap and laughed her high-pitched, strained laugh. She smelled sour.

That scene was jerking around in my head while I

galloped through the churchyard with Susu O'Gorman yelping and breathing heavily under my jacket. I could hear Mrs. O'Gorman's mad, tinkling laugh. The three of us, Decko, Ger and me, were also laughing by the time we reached the hideout. I thought it funnier still that Susu didn't understand what was so funny.

Susu was the male. Mrs. O'Gorman's other two dogs were bitches and we never knew their names. Susu was the friendliest. It was possible to stick your hand between the bars of the gate into Mrs. O'Gorman's garden, stroke his back and touch his pink tongue. The other two would back off and hide in the porch. So when Susu snapped and connected his teeth with Ger's fingers, the three of us realised instantly that Susu wasn't Susu.

"It's the wrong dog," I said. In my stomach I felt a foreign, wobbly feeling. I ripped off the balaclava I'd made from my old red woolly hat.

Ger walked rapidly around in small circles, shaking his hand and putting it under his armpit. Despite his obvious pain, he abruptly used his good hand to tear off the green bomber jacket tied round his waist and swung it at the Pekinese. The dog snarled the way a dwarf lawnmower might when fired into life. We backed off with fright, which seemed to frighten the dog. It scampered a few yards away, lay down and whimpered.

A low grunt behind our backs caused us to spin round. The explanation for the dog's sudden cowardice stood before us, his piercing eyes assessing the situation.

"It's not our dog," Ger said. "We're just bringing him for a walk."

Decko gave Ger a *leave it, say nothing* nudge with his elbow. "Take off your balaclava."

Ger pulled off his balaclava, one of his mother's stockings.

Geronimo Hawk looked about seven feet in height close up as he bent down and twisted his way through the trees, saplings and hanging brambles. He stared intensely at each of us. His eyes fascinated me. They were more like the eyes of a majestic bird of prey fixing on you a gaze of hatred from behind reinforced mesh wire. Just looking into his eyes and you could tell that he knew far more about you than you knew about him.

This was the first time we'd seen Geronimo that summer. He arrived every year round about the time when we were set free for three months from that stupid, green-walled kip I wish I could stop thinking about during the holidays.

Anyway, there we were, closer than we'd ever been to the Hawk outside of town, and we hadn't even known he was back for the summer. He held his head tilted back and his nose was crinkled.

In our eagerness to please him, we almost stumbled over each other to let him through the unintentional wall we'd created between him and the dog by huddling close together. He scooped the dog up in one large hand. The dog panted and a shiver ran from its head to tail like a small wave beneath its fur. The Hawk brought it close to his nostrils and inhaled deeply enough to make a noise. In the shade of the trees the dog's fur matched the colour of the Hawk's beard. It looked as if a dog grew out of his face.

Seemingly satisfied, the Hawk then placed the dog back on the ground and turned to go. I could feel an instant thaw take place in my frozen body. Decko and Ger looked equally relieved.

For my benefit, Ger made a silent 'phew' expression.

Geronimo Hawk then stopped with his back to us. Unconsciously, I'd been concentrating on the mucky and torn ends of the outfit he wore. People said he'd been a monk, and that's why he always wore a brown dress-yoke, like what monks wear. But people said lots of things.

Had he seen me staring at him? Maybe he sensed the picture in my head? Or had he smelt my laughter? A brief picture of him grasping me by the throat and raising me to his nose popped like a burst balloon at the sound of his voice.

"No more prayers," he said.

His voice was big but sounded different to other men's voices. More like the way an animal would speak if it could talk; an animal that growls.

We waited. He waited, too, for an answer maybe.

"I never pray," I said.

Decko tapped me on the thigh and indicated that I shut the fuck up.

"For thirty years," he went on, while taking a month to turn his body round again, "I called out to Him." He raised his arm palm up over his head and followed it with his eyes. "I asked Him what the grass was for." He swept a long arm over the earth. "Who owns the wind?"

You do," I said.

Decko clicked at me with his tongue, snapped his fingers and gave me one of those *you're-dead*-looks.

"Where does the daylight sleep?" he continued. "Is there a reason why a man shouldn't whisper?"

The Hawk paused, his attention shifting about him as though something might yet answer him.

"Too many questions," he said, "and no answers."

And then, like a startled beast, he left.

"What if he comes back?" Ger said, as we listened to the rustle and snap of the Hawk's retreat dissolve into a stuttering afterimage.

"Geronimo," he called out through the trees.

We echoed his yell. "Geronimo," we shouted.

The dog that wasn't Susu stood upright on its feet again now that Geronimo Hawk had left. Its legs were hidden beneath its light brown body wig. Panting laboriously, a pink, unfurled tongue lolled from its grinning mouth. Its flat, human baby face and huge eyes were filled to bursting with such accusation. I figured that we must have appeared to it like a bunch of Geronimo Hawks. In a couple of minutes I could only glance at it sideways.

"Okay, plan B," Decko said.

"We kill it?" Ger asked.

"Nobody said nothing definite about a plan B," I said.

"Stay cool, you guys," Decko said. "This is my definite plan B now. We bring the ransom down to a fiver."

Susu was Mrs. O'Gorman's favourite, so we guessed it quite reasonable that she wouldn't be as keen to pay out big money for the safe return of one of the bitches. After all, Mam had told us, Mrs. O'Gorman was someone who'd 'buried two husbands'. She was obviously tough, and if she didn't care about somebody too much, she'd just dig a hole and toss him in the ground. I pictured her standing over a perfectly rectangular black crater in her back garden working with a pick and shovel and laughing her faraway laugh beneath a full moon. Beside her lie the bodies of two old men next to a large mound of mucky earth.

"Aw, deadly, Decko, she likes you," Ger said about Susu's stand-in.

"Good girl," Decko said, as the dog rolled over onto her back and smiled back at him. "There's a good fiver. That's the girl. C'mon Fiver."

And Fiver, delighted with her new name, gave Decko her instant allegiance, as though she would have followed him forever. And so would I, if I could have.

But sometimes, even Decko got me pretty angry.

"No," I said, when he told Ger and me to stop stalling

and to take off to collect the ransom. “You said you’d do it.”

“Okay,” he said with a smile that forecast an oral whack to the side of the head. “She’s yours.” He motioned to hand me the thin piece of blue rope he’d attached to the dog’s collar.

Now whether Fiver was reacting to Ger standing next to me, I’ve always wondered about.

The flat-faced, hairy human baby crouched her oversized head to the ground, curled back its lips as much as excessive overbreeding would allow, and produced a nasally pneumatic snarl that snapped me from anger to cowardice.

“Hurry up,” Decko said, “and don’t come back without the money.”

The Pekinese gazed up at him and its sad, fluffy tail wagged violently. With no tails to wag or droop, we left.

While walking past the Grotto and the blue and white statue of Hail Mary next to the priests’ garden, I did what Mam had taught me to do. Looking up at the Hail Mary set high up in the rock face, I blessed myself and said, “Holy Mother of God, forgive me my terrible sins.”

Ger stopped walking and laughed one of his lazy laughs.

“What’s funny?” I asked, laughing with Ger anyway.

“I was just thinking,” he said.

“Yeah,” I said, expecting him to tell me, but he was working himself into one of his rare laughing fits. He kind of collapsed onto the grass, the heels of his hands pressed to his forehead and his body shaking in slow motion. Next he was on his back, his legs pedalling the air.

I dived on top of him. “C’mon, tell me,” I said, tickling him under his armpits. “What’s so funny?” But that just made him worse.

Suddenly exhausted, I lay back in the grass, the hot sun bathing my closed eyelids in blood.

Ger's faraway voice pulled me from an instantaneous torpor. He'd said something about Aller.

"It's the God honest truth."

"What is?"

"He said he'd like to give her one."

"Who did? What are you on about, Ger Flanigan?"

"Aller. Aller said he wouldn't mind giving Hail Mary one. Her being a virgin and all."

"What?"

"It's true." Ger did his impression of Decko doing his Aller impression, frowning and sticking out his lower lip. "I wouldn't mind giving her one," he said in Aller's thick-tongued voice. And he wagged and wiggled his tongue up at Hail Mary, his head to the side and his hands joined in prayer.

"Fuck off, Ger, you spa. You're sick."

"God forgive you," Ger said, in this little old woman's squeaky voice.

"Suck my dick," I said, which started us laughing again. "Hey, Hail Mary," I shouted up at the statue.

This pulled Ger from his laughter the way I knew it would. His eyes were as big as ten pence coins and his face bloated with expectation, daring me.

I hesitated, not yet sure if I had the balls to outdo even Aller and his scumbag mouth. But, like the unstoppable momentum that takes you when you run down a hill, turning back wasn't an option.

"Hey Mary," I repeated. "Hail Mary. How'd you like to suck on this?" I grabbed myself the way I'd seen skinners grab themselves, my hand clamped over my groin, and I made a Les Dawson face with sticky-out lips. "Suck my big, fat, baldy one," I roared at the blue and white effigy that ignored us from her perch in the man-made cliff face.

That got us roaring so hard, I kind of pissed myself a bit, but who cared? This happened before. The day was hot. My underpants would dry out.

What did silence the pair of us, though, was a high-pitched voice shouting from behind the tall hedge.

"You boys. You boys," the voice screeched. "You little blackguards. Wait until I talk to your mothers and fathers... When I get my hands on you..."

"The balaclavas," I said. "Quick." I pulled my woolly hat down over my face and shifted it so I could peer out through the holes I'd made for eyes.

"It's him," Ger said, dragging his mother's stocking out of his pocket.

"Who?" I whispered. "Geronimo Hawk?" knowing it sounded absolutely nothing like the Hawk.

"No, you moron. The Pet-rest."

The older boys, the ones who had the priest for religious classes, had given the priest his nickname.

The hedge was very thick and was taller than the priest. It was about thirty yards to the entrance in the hedge that led into the vegetable garden. We were young and I was fast and knew it. I often raced buses from one stop to another and won.

"Run," I said, half-consciously wondering why we hadn't taken off the second the Pet-rest's slithery voice shrieked into the evening.

We took off like a couple of collie pups released from a kennel. Strewn around the ground beneath us were half-grown pears that had fallen from the trees above. I slipped on a pear but righted myself.

We'd made it around the perimeter of the church's curved fence, but the clomp, clomp of the priest's heeled and capped brogues told us he was determined to catch us. We often heard the older boys talking about how the Pet-rest was always chasing after young fellows, so we knew he had plenty of practice. But refuge was now just paces ahead. There were stacks of places to hide in the side roads off the large shop-filled street, which was the centre of our town.

Before reaching the shops, something completely unexpected happened. A sickening burning sensation welled up inside my stomach. My head felt dizzier than it would have had I been spinning on the spot for five minutes. Large black dots, perfectly round, jerked across my eyes and disappeared. I don't know if I called out to Ger to help me, but next he was crouched down beside me behind the garden wall I'd stumbled over, pressing me gently to the earth.

I dragged off the balaclava and used it to towel my sweaty face.

Ger normally didn't say too much unless he had something definite to say, but now he was totally silent. And, although my senses were too cloudy and my vision in particular too blurred, I knew he was indicating that the Pet-rest was near and that we couldn't breathe.

But now that the burning ache in my insides was subsiding and the shadows before my eyes had lifted enough to allow me to make out the pink and white geraniums in which we were lying, my entire being was hijacked suddenly by a thirst that no amount of water could ever slake. Oxygen, not liquid, was what I craved.

Panic clutched me by the throat. I tried to inhale deeply, but the suffocating fingers gripped my neck tighter with every attempted inhalation until my windpipe seemed blocked and I would burn up. And then the garden gate creaked open. We were nabbed.

"What are you two rascals doing?" a voice sweeter than I could've thought possible asked.

Without realising it, I was breathing naturally again and

my senses were as sharp as a carnivore's canine. A girl Ger and me had never seen before that day stood on the garden path with her hands on her hips. She smiled a smile from a mouth so crammed with big white teeth, I felt like crying. I couldn't say why. She looked like a small adult.

"This is my house," she said. "Do you two want to have a picnic with me around there?"

We craned our necks to look towards the rear garden, turned back to look at each other and then back at the girl and nodded our eagerness. That was how I first met Sarah Fernandez.

"What happened to your nose?" I asked her and deliberately touched what looked like a fine scar across its bridge.

She stuck out her lower lip and turned her huge green eyes inwards like Clarence, the cross-eyed lion, as though she were trying to see the mark for the first time.

"I like playing with boomerangs," she said, and exaggerated her smile to show me that it was a smile crease from bunching up the muscles in her face, the way some adults had smiling lines around their eyes.

A muscular white and brown Jack Russell dog sprinted towards us from the house. The significance of this four-legged reminder registered instantly.

"Decko," I roared. "We forgot about Decko." I pushed myself away from the table but my chair remained stuck to the ground like it had grown roots, while the table tipped over, spilling Sarah's carefully prepared picnic to the ground.

"C'mon Ger, let's scarper." And we took off to the sound of Sarah screaming at us mingled with the confused growling-bark of the Jack Russell torn between his instinct to pursue the cowardly-fleeing taking second place to remaining and devouring the culinary delights scattered on the grass before him.

So we were on the move again, pounding along the main street, charging past the church, brazenly flinging a few expletives at the invisible Pet-rest, and ripping through the narrowing road for home.

"Decko will kill us," I coughed out between quickened breathing and loud gasps for air.

"She's really pretty," Ger said through equally laboured breathing.

"Shut up, Ger." And I pulled him to the ground by leaping onto his back while we were both still in full flight. "There's Decko."

Decko was outside old Mrs. O'Gorman's front gate and talking to someone inside the garden hidden by the pillar. Ger and me were too far away to hear their voices clearly. We played possum for a moment, lying half on a grassy verge, until Ger rolled over and asked me to get off him. But in the same breath he wondered if Sarah had a boyfriend.

I slid back on top of him, looked into his unfocused eyes and felt the instant urge to pound in his face with my fists. He must have picked up on something in my countenance, or felt my body stiffen maybe, because he twisted himself over so he was on his stomach.

"Raz, let me up will you?" His tone of self-pity succeeded only in making me want to pick up a thin piece of broken plastic piping next to the kerb and use it to crack him across the back of the head.

"I didn't do nothing," he said. "It's not my fault, Susu or the shagging Pet-rest."

"Shut your stupid mouth," I said, and I warned him not to move as I was leaning over to grasp the piece of piping.

I screamed out in pain when a large foot pressed my fingers, wrapped around the piping, into the ground.

A blinding yellow belt of sunshine, a streak of blue sky, Aller O'Callahan's gruff voice, his large silhouette and the sickeningly familiar smell of cooked meat from his sweaty hands, crowded my senses as he dragged me to my feet.

Aller's chuckling died when Decco's voice boomed through the street like a car crash.

"Aller, you're dead," he said. And I could hear his black boots tearing towards us.

He released me instantly. A switch might have been flicked. I fell to the ground, crumpled and without strength, my head crashed to the earth. But I was conscious yet. This was it, the confrontation that was written, and the clash that had to be. Decko in a fight with Aller, and I was there to witness it, the bout of my childhood, and perhaps my life.

But that fight, like all the great bouts and battles, was to have a lead-up-to period. The sweet voice I'd last heard screaming at Ger and me sounded for the first time in our street.

"Who's that?" Decko said, transfixed on the owner of the voice calling to us without shouting.

"It's her," Ger said. "It's Sarah."

I forced myself to sit up. Ger broke into an impromptu Indian war dance, but stopped just as promptly before she reached us. Placing his upstretched arms on Decko's shoulders, he added, "She's come," in a way that suggested we'd all been waiting for her forever but never actually believed in her arrival.

"Get away from me," Decko said, sweeping Ger aside a bit too forcefully.

Sarah Fernandez's quick and determined pace slackened at about three or four houses away. The confident adult-girl from the picnic in the back garden was gone. In its wake was a stereotypical pre-pubescent girl, giggling into her hand and looking at Decko sideways as she advanced clearly towards him on spindly legs.

"Hi," she said to Decko alone.

"Howdy Ma'am," he replied, and doffed an imaginary cowboy hat.

"Would you like to kiss me?"

"What?" He visibly gulped.

"Kiss me?" she repeated, and tilted her head upwards and to the side, her tongue pressing into her cheek.

You could see Decko trawling for a witty response, but all he succeeded in doing was to simper and look from Ger to me to Aller.

"Go on, Decko," Ger said, "kiss her."

Aller was making a long high-pitched note in his throat that must have been approval, because his eyes were creased and his mouth was twisted.

"No," Decko said. "I mean yes, I would, but I have to go now. What's your name? Not that I care anyways…"

"Good," she said, "'cause I don't want to kiss you"

Before any of us knew how to react to Sarah's game, if it was a game, she stepped up to Ger instead, and kissed him quickly on the cheek, then half-pirouetted in slow motion and rested her open gaze on me. Remembering the pain I'd forgotten about, I massaged my throat and did what I felt was a convincing impression of someone undergoing great torture but too strong-willed to moan about it.

"Raz Richardson," she said, as if she'd just noticed me. I was content to know that she'd remembered my name. She pursed her lips and scrunched up her face to show she was considering what to say.

"What's your favourite colour?" she asked in a way that sounded like a trick question. Give the wrong answer and she mightn't kiss me the way she'd kissed Ger.

So instead I frowned at her red shoes and prayed hard to God that she'd just kiss me. *Please Holy God make her kiss me. C'mon, please, make her kiss me.*

"Blue," Aller said in answer to Sarah's question to me. "Me favourite colour is blue. Definite."

"Who asked you, Aller?" I said, expecting Decko to jump in and back me up the way he always did when Dad or anybody else was messing me around. Might as well have expected John Wayne to gallop into the street on a white horse.

Decko's face looked stupid. His mouth was open and his lower teeth were scratching at his upper lip, while his eyes, staring at Sarah, were as big as those bush baby yokes I saw in a nature programme.

What I noticed next gave me the first doubt I can ever remember having about my sexuality. Looking up at Sarah from where I sat on the ground, I noticed what I'd seen before but hadn't really noticed: on the backs of her arms were dark, black hairs, far thicker than mine.

I felt a tingling itch below my stomach. She was hairier than Geronimo Hawk, and I'd been praying she'd kiss me. An even greater hunger to lean forward and squash my mouth to Sarah's somersaulted inside my stomach, when I saw that under her nose was a wispy moustache, stronger at the corners of her mouth.

"I like red," Ger said. "I'm going to have a red Ferrari someday."

"No you're not, Ger Flanigan," I said. I leapt to my feet. "I am. You know that."

But I didn't really care too much about the way Ger chose my favourite stupid colour and car. I just wanted to shout away the idea that I fancied a girl who was more like a boy, with her moustache and hairy arms, and probably legs, too.

I pulled Ger from the small group, but in a way that he'd know I wasn't mad at him. He smiled his expectant smile, and darted a glance behind us to see if they were trying to listen to us.

"Did you see the hair on her arms?" I said.

"Hair? On her arms?"

"Shit, Ger, why can't you ever whisper?"

Aller, who was standing nearest us, obviously did hear what I hoped Sarah hadn't. He sniggered and did a poor mime of an ape behind Sarah's back. She caught him at that moment he threw a quick glance behind to see if his audience was laughing.

"I've got to go now," she said. She looked at the ground. "I think I left the gate to the back garden open. Jackie will escape."

Decko held up his hand to Aller as Sarah skulked off without saying goodbye. Aller met Decko's high five as though they'd successfully executed a pact they'd made earlier.

But being able to figure Decko out wasn't the same as understanding him.

"Aller, your old man's looking for you," one of Aller's young neighbours called to him from the top of the street.

"Me dinner," Aller said. Off he bounded.

Our mam wasn't so strict about mealtimes, but we took off too. Mam wasn't a great cook either, but the food tasted better hot than cold.

A trillion things ricocheted around in my head on the way back to our house. We'd bungled the kidnap of Susu, and hadn't even managed yet to get half the original ransom. Decko told us we'd get it later.

"But, but…" I said.

"But fucking nothing," Decko said. "I'm starved. And I'm pissed off, right?"

I went back into my head and got to thinking that if the Pet-rest had recognised Ger and me, even though we had on our balaclavas, we were dead if he told our parents what we'd said about Hail Mary.

Added to these disasters was my disillusionment with Decko because he seemed to have chickened out of fighting Aller. But if Decco was feeling any sense of shame over his cowardly climb-down, he gave no appearance of it. He strutted along in front of me in his usual way, covering about ten yards in a stride. Every few yards Ger made a running skip to keep up with him.

Woven into my thoughts was Sarah Fernandez's face and the silky sound of her name. Despite all the confusion I was experiencing, because of everything that had happened so far that day, thinking about Sarah made me feel strange. The crease in her nose, the unusual green colour of her eyes, the hurt look that came into those eyes when Aller made fun of her, and even the wispy little moustache and the dark hairs on her thin arms; or, maybe, especially because of her hairiness, an insatiable hunger lodged itself deep within me. I felt hollow, and the hollowness rose to my throat in spasms. Was this what it felt like to be in love?

There was another thought emerging out of all of this. It insinuated itself on me like something evil that you don't want to accept but whose existence is unavoidable. Sarah Fernandez's hairiness made her more like a boy than a girl. This meant that the strange feelings she aroused in me made me something that would make Ger and Ladders and all the kids in school treat me as though I were a freak. Decko, too, would hate me and not want to be my brother anymore. Fancying a girl who was hairier than a boy probably made me gay.

I didn't eat too much at teatime. Thinking about my new discovery made me sick.

After tea Decko said he was in a hurry. He wanted to get back to finish off the oil painting he was making to enter into the Texaco Art Competition. Decko always said 'making a picture', never 'paint'. He said it was better if just the two of us went back to get Fiver. I pleaded with him to let me call for Ger. He relented, but the delay got him kind of angry. So when Ger started questioning him on the way back to the fields about how come he left the dog in the valley by itself, Decko turned on him.

"What's it to you?" Decko said.

"Nothing," Ger said.

"Anyway," Decko said, and stared at the ground. "The Hawk came back. I thought he wanted the place to himself for a while."

"You're a chicken," Ger said, laughing.

"Shut your mouth, tortoise-boy," Decko said.

Ger said he was sorry and only messing, but Decko was pretty angry now. I knew it was best to say nothing for a while.

Suddenly, Decko was in an even greater hurry. "Move," he said. "You're too slow."

Ger and me did as Decko ordered. We trotted ahead of him. I never looked around until we were back in the valley.

"Decko," I said at the river. I'm parched. I need a drink."

"You can't drink out of that," he said. There's dead cats and bottles and all kinds of crap in there."

"I don't care."

"Me too," Ger said.

The mucky ground at the edge of the river soaked into my jeans as I knelt down. It felt cool and good. I scooped up the freezing water in my hands and slaked my thirst. Ger was still drinking when I'd finished.

"C'mon, you pair of thicks," Decko said.

On we went.

We were nearing the old cowshed by a bend in the river when we heard the distinctive sound of someone moving through the high weeds and around the blackberry bushes ahead of us. We stopped. Geronimo Hawk. It had to be. He was coming towards us, his heavy breathing growing louder. To flee then was an admission of cowardice, and it would put future escapades into the fields in jeopardy. The three of us must have known this instinctively.

"Aller," Decko said. "It's not him, it's Aller."

"Scarper," Aller said, as he pounded along the pathway towards us. "The Hawk. The Hawk is coming."

"Is he chasing you or what, Aller?" Decko asked.

But, like a startled fox, Aller disappeared into the undergrowth that crowded the twisted and overgrown cattle run that wended its way back to the church.

"He looked really scared," Ger said.

"What was Aller doing here anyway?"

Decko guessed Aller must have been trailing us earlier when we took the dog from Mrs. O'Gorman's home. He then ordered us to be quiet while he listened. We all three listened. Nothing: just the sound of the birds and the bleating of sheep; but not for long.

"Geronimo." The Hawk sounded quite far away.

"Don't answer him," Decko said.

"Geronimo," the Hawk repeated.

Could be that it's the distance of time and hindsight. Yet, I think it seemed to me then that I heard what Decko must have heard. The Hawk's roar had a new note to it. One I'd never heard before. I felt that roar like a kind of angry sea beating on a cliff face. It exhilarated and unnerved me.

With Decko's lead, we pushed on.

At the bottom of Hikers' Hill, the place where, Decko told us, he had left Fiver, there was no sign of the dog.

"Where the hell is she?" Decko asked.

"Maybe she ran away," I said.

"The Hawk could have eaten her," Ger said.

"Shut up," Decko said. "I tied her to that branch."

The Hawk's call bellowed out again, echoing around the valley. It sounded farther off. He was moving away from us.

"Where's he calling from?" Ger said. "It's hard to tell."

"Look," I said. "Up there."

At the top of Hikers' Hill was an old tree, long since dead, which had been hit by lightning. Its bony-fingered branches stretched skyward. And something, too far from us to make out, was caught in its clawed hand.

"We'll go check it," Decko said.

The steep walk up Hikers' Hill was long and tiring. As we neared the top we saw her. Her lifeless body swung gently in the summer breeze. Her eyes were already glassing over, but seemed to stare at us still.

Somebody had taken the piece of rope Decko used as a makeshift lead for Susu O'Gorman's stand-in and hanged the dog from a low bough.

Inoffensive seeming, and yet not, Aller O'Callaghan's baseball bat lay hidden in the nearby nettles. Three days would pass before Decko found the bat and cajoled us into returning with him to witness his discovery. Hikers' Hill, from then on and through our childhood years, what was left of them, was the place of The Hanging Tree.

In the meantime, before Decko discovered Aller's baseball bat, we pinned Fiver's murder on someone who, for all of us, was the obvious killer: Geronimo Hawk. Without discussing it too much, we walked resignedly home, and neither Decko nor me said goodbye to Ger when he left us for his home.

Fiver's death, and the way she died, was unreal and unacceptable. Far better I found was to try and convince myself of anything else. I lay in bed that night without sleeping, wanting instead, only to be responsible for one of

Mrs. O'Gorman's bug-eyed babies lost and wailing somewhere in the lonely night.

Far off, in the shivery solitude of night-time, I thought I heard a dog howling a demonic plea to the darkness. I jerked the blankets covering me away, got out of bed, pulled on my runners and a pullover and climbed out the bedroom window to the drainpipe and shinnied up onto the roof of the house.

A heavy sleeper, Decko slept on. Besides, he was used to me climbing on to the roof.

The flat ladder, used for replacing slates, which had been in place always, was wet and slimy with dew-covered moss. I gripped it tightly and felt my pyjama bottoms soaking up the sodden cold. The discomfort would be temporary. When I went back inside, I could change out of my pyjamas into my Adidas tracksuit.

Resting against the chimney pot, and holding on to the TV aerial attached to it, I felt the darkness wash away the hurt in my head. The particular oak trees in my head were the ones Decko had 'made' in an oil painting he gave Mam for her birthday. The trees were the background to a painting he had done with him and me as little kids.

I remained on the rooftop of the house long enough to hear the milkman's screaming engine turning into our street. The milkman's confident melodic whistling filled the air when the milk float's engine died.

It fascinated me to study how the milkman clutched about ten bottles of milk in his arms and hands while he deposited them between three houses. He seemed to sense me looking at him when he bounced up our driveway with five pint bottles of milk glued to one hand. He craned his neck to look around the garden and behind him, but, obviously, never considered looking up.

Resuming his whistling, he shrugged his shoulders, and kind of skipped back to his truck.

More a feeling than a thought, I always felt that one day I'd turn out to be like the milkman, a creature that belonged to the morning, the way birds did, and rabbits, too, while everyone else was still asleep in bed.

Downing Out in New York

Nobody believed me. Most of them ignored me. Just breezed by like I wasn't there. A few, wearing tentative smiles, listened while I tried to tell them my story. Occasionally, they gave me some quarters or a couple of dollars. The odd one would even give me a *hang in there, buddy* tap on the shoulder or back. And that's what I did. I kept at it. What else could I do? I wasn't the one to blame for this.

"Excuse me, sir. Ahem, I need to get to Boston. It's an emergency. I was mugged. Five or six guys jumped me. Lost everything. I have relatives in Boston." I cringed at the lies I heard spilling from my own mouth, but the actual truth sounded far too unlikely.

That bitch. I didn't want to think about it. Futility. Wasted energy. I had to get myself out of this. Track her down. Get back what she took from me. Keep moving forward.

New York's finest helped me to keep moving.

"But, officer," I pleaded, when I was warned I'd get done for loitering and begging. "I'm Irish. My passport's been stolen. And my papers. There was a whole gang of them. Puerto Ricans. They had knives and baseball bats. I was touring the States and…" I liked to change the story. I figured it would help me buy time.

"Well you better get going so," the cop said. "You won't see nothing standing in the same place. You'll get your boots stole right out from under you."

The cops were funny guys. They liked to joke and stuff. But the thing is, you couldn't trust them. You couldn't trust anybody. I learned that fast. Just two days after this thing happened, this old guy starts talking to me in the park. I was trying to tune into the birds' singing when he sits down right next to me on a bench early in the morning. There were empty benches everywhere, and he sits down on my bench.

"Won't be long now," he said. He was looking straight ahead. I thought he was some old crazy talking to himself. "The daffodils," he goes on. "They're the first that'll pop up." He made a wheezy chuckling sound. "Then the tulips." He twisted his whole body toward me. My stomach did a somersault looking at him. His face was a net of scabs, and the skin that wasn't scabby was as grey as his beard.

"Right," I said. I unfolded the newspaper I'd taken from a bin and pretended to be engrossed in how the euro was faring against the U.S. dollar.

"How long you been on the streets?" he asked.

"Me?" An instant rage bubbled inside my head. "I'm travelling, you know, hitch-hiking across the country. I come from Ireland."

I stopped myself telling this old git that I had a degree in music performance. Why was I explaining myself to this old man?

"The best thing to do is to stay put," he said. "Keep your head down. That's what I do. Nobody bothers you."

The wind shifted and a vomity, rubbish bin hum lifted off the old lad. I affected a blank stare at the middle of the pond for a few seconds, and then I dropped my head back into the newspaper. Despite his situation, the bum seemed sharp enough. He'd get the message.

People were beginning to fill up the benches nearby. I half-cupped a hand over my face, like I was shielding my eyes from the sun. There was no sun. If the old lad had confused me for one of his own, ordinary people would too. But how could they? Okay, I'd slept in a skip down an alleyway for the past two nights. In the skip was paper and office stuff. I mean it was a clean skip, and it had a roof and everything. I broke the lock. Just pulled up the lid and got in. I slept all right, considering. And my clothes were no different to every other guy my age on the street: jeans and T-shirt, a dark T-shirt. Was there something obvious about my face? I don't mean anything heavy or telling in my countenance that gave me away, but something obvious other than a few days beard growth. Grime maybe. I needed to see my reflection.

"Can you keep an eye on this bag for a minute?" I asked the old man.

He had his head on his chest now and his eyes were closed. He appeared to be asleep. I left the bag on the bench and hurried across to the pond. Leaving the bag sitting there was a way of holding on to my seat. I wasn't too pushed anyway, because generally people avoided sitting next to homeless guys.

Through the lightly rippled surface on the pond I looked as I imagined I would: tired, five o'clock shadowed and tanned. And my hair looked tidy. I've always had a tight cut. Overall I looked like any guy you'd see in the street.

I scooped up some water with one hand and worked my fingers over my face and into my scalp. It felt good. Kind of cleared up a lot of things that had been muzzy. Who needed a jealous girlfriend anyway? Somebody who'd deliberately put temptation in your way, using one of her own friends to test your fidelity, deserved what she got. She's the kind of bitch who's only happy when she's unhappy. How I ever got stuck with her in the first place I can't answer. It's as though she had it all planned from the start. Take me to the States to meet her mom and dad, do a road trip, the two of us, manoeuvre things so my visa runs out and I have to stay here, orchestrate the little charade with her best buddy, a girl designed by nature to bring out the animal in any normal man, come upon us unexpectedly and, bada-bing, as they say here, I'm reversing into the night-time with faulty brakes.

She goes hysterical, screaming and shouting and clawing at me with those red nails. Even attacks her friend. And this is all going on in the hotel room. She threatens to call the authorities right there and then. She'll tell them I'm an illegal alien. It all happens in seconds. She picks up the phone receiver and starts stabbing at the dial pad. I kind of lose it and smash the phone off the bedside table, only it catches her in the ribs. She lets out this extended scream. One of those screams you hear in movies. Now she's bitching about assault and screaming louder. I pull on the clothes I'd been wearing, grab my bag, and am on the road. No car, no wallet and no violin.

I go back to the hotel the next day, but the guy in reception gets real ticked-off when I keep pressing him about the violin. I figured she'd have taken the wallet, no question, but she knows how I am about my music. She must have left it, I insist. He keeps up this nasty smile and repeats, in this barely tolerating voice, how the bill was paid and the room vacated that morning. No violin was found in the room. The manager is equally unhelpful.

An adventure, that's what it was, I told myself, before twisting around and heading back to the bench. Something to tell the folks back home, if I ever got back home. And then I saw them – one on either side of my bag. Another iffy-looking character in filthy beige slacks and an angry, purple complexion was sitting where I'd been sitting. He and the old bum were engaged in a conversation that sounded like a growling match. And my holdall, they'd shifted it. I stomped over to them, ready for action. The two old grizzlies stopped talking and watched my approach.

"I asked you to keep your eye on my bag, not touch it, didn't I?" I said, addressing the old bum. The yanks are right. That's what they are. *Bums*.

"Take it easy, pal," the purple one said. He held up

splayed fingers and moved his hands the way a conductor indicates a diminuendo.

"Hey, mister," I said into the gnarled face of the first bum. "I'm talking to you." Emptied of supposed recognition, his red eyes slid past me and locked onto a flock of pigeons on the ground a couple of benches away squabbling over breadcrumbs.

I ripped open the zip and started rooting inside, making a real show of it. "If anything is missing from here, I'm going to kill you," I heard myself bellowing. But immediately I was sorry for my outburst. I reminded myself of *her* and her hysterics. And when I found everything that should be there – the tin box with the few dollars and coins I'd gotten from people on the street, my watch with the broken strap, and an address book – I wanted to apologise to the old guy, but something wouldn't let me. Instead I shook my head disapprovingly while closing the bag, as though I was still miffed about it being interfered with, and limped away. I didn't have a limp, but sometimes my body does things without consulting my head.

Not until I was a good forty minutes away from the park and back in the city did I discover that I'd been on the money in my suspicions about the old guy. My water. That filthy hobo had swiped my bottle of water. Almost full it was, too. It never would have occurred to me before just how big a deal it is to have a bottle of water with you when you're running solo on the streets. I'd taken it for granted, a lot like the way I'd gotten used to having a girlfriend around me.

Apart from needing to wash away the miniature Sahara in my throat, the bottle was a kind of crutch, something to hold onto when I approached strangers and pitched my story. Made me look legitimate, I thought, a beat-up traveller doing his thing. Now I had to break into the few dollars given me on the street. That way I'd never get the fare to Boston to *her* parents' house. Once I made it to her parents' place, even if she wasn't there, they'd fix me up with a replacement instrument. They're good people. You could tell that right off. They'd understand. Soon as I had a violin again, I could start busking and make some real money, get myself cleaned up, and maybe even book into a hotel.

After the cop told me to push on, I went to a shopping mall. Two security staff tailed me and openly walkie-talkied each other about my movements. I bought a giant packet of potato chips and six small bottles of water, before slipping back into the city's endless avenues and towering skyscrapers. Concentrating on my own tatty white runners, I avoided the faces passing in the streets, and only looked up when, by default, I found the little shop I'd been hunting for. The streets of New York are a maze.

In the large shop window the saxophones and trumpets caught splinters of neon and sparkled. A trio of shiny guitars flaunted themselves like beauties from a Rubens' canvas. My interest lay farther in at the back of the shop where I could just about make out other stringed instruments. I'd been inside the shop a number of times that week already, but now I hesitated.

The rising smell coming off my body, an oniony-garlicy stink, wouldn't make me feel any better about myself in the shop's enclosed space. I belched. A cloying fishy aftertaste from the scampi-flavoured crisps was in my mouth. I gulped down a mouthful of water. My vision focused on my reflection in the shop window. Weather-beaten, my skin had turned red, almost purple. The five-o'clock shadow was now a full-blown tawny beard, and my hair was already growing. Bits of it stuck up like I'd shoved my finger into a cartoon socket. I moved on into the day.

“That bitch. That stupid bitch,” I snarled at the dizzying pavement.

A group of teenage girls I had to walk around giggled loudly after me. I sensed the eyes of other passers-by slashing at me. I increased my walking pace. What the hell were they looking at? Dumb-asses. How many of them had been to college? Did they ever play in an orchestra at a national concert hall?

I watched an old woman approaching at a distance. She was shuffling along on a cane and mumbling to a tiny dog she had on a lead. As she came closer I could see what she was doing. Pretending not to notice me, trying to keep her wrinkled old eyes averted, it was so obvious. Who did she think she was with her black headscarf and uppity attitude? Even the dog ignored me.

I stopped and barked, “Hey, missus.”

The old woman made a squeak of supposed fright and looked about her as though I were invisible.

“Here I am, missus,” I said, and I flapped my arms like a chicken.

She squinted at me through lenses as thick as a telephone directory, looked me up and down, and then turned into the traffic on the busy road. Cars beeped and drivers roared at her. I joined them.

“It won’t be long now,” I bellowed into cupped hands. “Pretty soon the daffodils will be poking their noses out of the ground.” The sound of my own voice alarmed me greatly. It could’ve been someone else’s voice. There was a rawness in it, a deep gravelish sound like a growl. But I wouldn’t let the old woman get away with her impertinence. I pointed after her retreating old carcass, rocked back and forth on the balls of my feet, and whinnied with laughter.

His Father's Son

He had expected it to be different. The daylight was as searing and radiant as midday on an open prairie. There should have been thunderclouds and torrential rain.

The red-bricked houses were a coppery-yellow. Marvelling at the houses caused a painful sensation in his chest, as though he had regained something he imagined had been lost forever. In the streets everyone seemed so happy. Even those who blessed themselves as the procession wheeled by barely let go of their smiles. And, apart from feeling relieved, wasn't he supposed to feel some other way?

Stopped at a set of traffic lights, he found himself concentrating on a tough looking youth crossing the road in front of their car. The youth's white sweatshirt was turned inside out. It was obvious. The black label at the back of the sweatshirt was clearly visible.

A ridiculous spectacle; had nobody drawn the boy's attention to this oversight? How could his mother or his friends allow him to walk around in public with his top inside out?

"Is Grandad watching me from heaven now, Dad?" Tommy asked from the rear seat.

"What?" he said. "Oh yeah, sure he is, Tommy. Grandad is looking down on you and your brother."

What was he doing? What kind of a son was he? His own father, the boys' grandfather, dead in the wooden box in the car ahead of them, and he was worrying about some kid's jumper turned inside out. He leaned his head out the window, an unconscious habit, and glanced at his own reflection in the wing mirror. Despite the heat blasting at his face through the open window, sinister fingernails clawed at the back of his neck.

His face was his father's face. The face his father wore in the wedding photographs, before he put on weight: those dark, probing eyes with a hint of surprise in them, the high forehead and thinning hairline.

Even the smell that morning from his electric razor, a deep smoky-brown smell, belonged to his father. The smell he remembered his father having when he took him fishing when he was small. Very small. Long before that smell turned sour. An indescribable smell, no, stench, something evil that the boys commented on, which made him ashamed to visit the house he grew up in. Was this what awaited him – his father's personal odour?

Already, earlier in the week, on one of the last of those inconvenient and endless trips to the hospital, his two old aunts, his father's sisters, had made their usual remarks. Aunt Penny started it. "Jack will live on in Charles," she said. "There's no doubt."

"The spit of him," Aunt Maggie agreed. "Right down to the teeth in his head. Look it." And she got him to open his mouth and smile at whoever was standing nearby to prove her point. His father – Jack, to his aunts – lay unconscious on his dying bed. Although Charles suspected he was awake, listening and judging without comment, as he had known him to do all his life.

Starting tomorrow Charles would grow a beard, grey hairs and all. His father detested beards. "Never trust a man with a beard," his father said a million times. "He's hiding behind it. There's something rotten about a man with a beard."

And Charles's father stuck to his principled belief right to the end. Despite the heavy drinking and the shabby clothes, he never allowed a beard to take hold. Even when he seemed incapable of clutching a razor in his shaky hands, when he hadn't the strength to use a corkscrew, and sometimes smashed the top off a wine bottle over the mantelpiece, he managed to shave himself; at least every other day.

Getting out of the car at the church, Charles readied himself for the predictable questions. He was glad to have the boys with him as a distraction.

"Tommy, take Jamie's hand," he said. "Good boy. Hold his hand, Jamie."

As they walked across the car park to the church, he was aware of feeling so much a part of everything around them. Through the warmed air he inhaled the sweet smell left by freshly mowed grass. Woven through the grassy fragrance was a humming chorus played by what appeared to be quite a swarm of bumblebees working a flowerbed of red tulips.

"Look, Daddy, look," Jamie said. "Mr. Bumbles."

"Yes, pet," he said. "We'll see them after. We have to go into Holy God's house first."

He tried to tune into a watery melody made by a bird he couldn't identify, but a neighbour he hardly spoke to, coming towards him at a walking pace that was almost a run, reminded him of his role. Letting go of Tommy's hand, he manoeuvred the two boys in front of him, rested a hand on each of their shoulders and waited.

The neighbour spoke before he reached him. "Charles," he shouted, with his hand outstretched in front of him halfway across the car park. "I'm real sorry for your troubles."

Charles smiled through what he hoped came across as a suitably mournful expression and lifted his own hand from Tommy's shoulder.

"Thank you," he said. "Thanks." He shook Mr. Ledwich's hand. He couldn't remember Ledwich's first name.

"Bert," Mr. Ledwich said. "Bertie Ledwich. Sorry for your troubles," he repeated.

"Thank you, Bert," Charles said. "Thanks, Bertie."

"These are the two boys then?" Ledwich said. He shook Tommy's hand and ruffled Jamie's hair. Charles smoothed Jamie's hair back into shape. "So," the neighbour went on, his eyes shifting about the car park. "Where's the good wife? Where's, em, Mrs. McGuire?"

"Oh, Catherine," Charles said, as though he hadn't expected the enquiry. "Cathy couldn't make it. It's her mother. She's not the best this weather."

Bertie Ledwich nodded like a horse. "I see," he said.

"Cathy's gone to look after her for a bit," Charles heard himself adding, although he had told himself he wasn't going to lie too much. Nobody's business.

"Terrible," Ledwich said. "It all comes together at once." He sucked in his lips and creased his eyes. "A sad, sad time in life." He dropped his eyes to the boys, shook his head, looked back up and reached for Charles's hand again. "Sorry for your troubles."

"Appreciate it," Charles said.

Bertie Ledwich backed away waving, nearly tripped into the flowerbed, steadied himself, smiled at his own clumsiness, and gave a final wave. A wave someone might give from a boat as they set sail to begin a new life in Australia.

By the time they were settled in the church, Charles was cringing inwardly over the three different versions he'd given to people asking him about Cathy's absence. Only two people in the church knew the truth. And one of them was dead.

Cathy was staying away, she had decided, because, if she attended the funeral of 'that man', she didn't know if she could stop herself from spitting into his grave, or worse. Charles understood. The memories of his father's ways he was struggling to forget wouldn't leave him alone.

The earliest incident Charles could remember went

back to when he was about ten or eleven. In a way the recollection always affected him worse than all the other recollections, because his father seldom drank back then.

Charles, a non-drinker, never accepted inebriation as mitigation for anything. And, yet, he often reasoned to himself, how part of him, an unconscious part, must have excused his father his intolerable behaviour in later years.

Listening to the priest throw out the usual eulogies, the type of thing he had heard bestowed on other dead men during funerals he had attended, Charles remembered a very different man. The priest spoke about Jack, the family man who, despite his human frailties, had overcome his weaknesses and made huge sacrifices to feed, clothe and keep his family in good health. The priest equated Jack's sacrifices with the very sacrifices made by the Son of God.

Charles, who was expected to say a few words about his father after the priest, tried to locate some of the qualities the priest spoke about in relation to his father. After all, Charles's mother had always argued, if you searched for something bad about someone, you'd find it. Better then to remember a person's good side was her Christian outlook.

An instant itchiness in Charles's scalp fought for supremacy with invisible crawling legs quick-marching under his shirt and around his back.

What good side? The man the priest was speaking about from the altar belonged to fiction, something that originated in a sermon.

Charles looked sideways and down at his two boys, Tommy, seven, and Jamie, an inquisitive three-year-old. Their bright-eyed, shining faces, untouched by cynicism, must have been the way he looked that day when he first realised that his father, the man whose large hand enveloped his on those days when they walked down the pier together with their fibre-glass fishing rods, was capable of callous betrayal against his own son.

Over thirty years later and that day had lost none of its disturbing impact.

Summertime. The Seventies. June or July. Charles and his older sister no longer played together. At fourteen, she considered herself too big to have her stupid little brother trailing around with her and her friends. A solitary boy by nature, Charles had one real friend, an undersized kid two years his junior whose own peers regarded as someone to play tricks on. Charles and the younger boy drifted together the way most of Charles's friendships happened throughout his life, including his marriage.

On the particular day in question, however, his friend was away on holidays with his family. This left Charles at a loose end.

He considered going up to the fields on the outskirts of town, but on your own would be no fun. Besides, there might be skinheads. There were always skinheads. Instead he kicked a ball around the streets until it got mad hot. He smelled the tar on the roads melting beneath the afternoon sun. His bare arms were getting red and he could feel a stinging sensation. Like nettle rash only different. And in his throat Charles had what his grandad described as a feeling of being *parched.* He needed a drink. But in order to get an ice-cold bottle of Coke or Fanta, he needed money.

Unlike the kids of Charles's children's generation, nobody had money back then for all the stuff yet to be invented – iPods, computer games, MP3s – let alone the price of a Coke. If you wanted something, you had to earn it.

On his bike, Charles set about a tour of the bins and skips at the sides and backs of local businesses and factories. His quest to secure enough money-back bottles yielded only a couple of scurvy-looking bottles, one of which was chipped. Making sure nobody was about, he smashed the bottles down a laneway and flew home on his purple chopper.

His mam was in bed with one of her crippling headaches. She asked him to leave her alone. Perfect. He went back downstairs and directly to his mam's handbag on the sideboard. His intention was to take a few coins from her purse, just the price of a can of Coke. A heart-sinking discovery awaited him.

There was no loose change in her purse. So, instead, he slipped out the one note from the back compartment, a five-pound note, and whizzed off to the shops. He opted for a bottle of Fanta over the Coke.

Outside the shop Charles sat atop his chopper, his feet on the pedals, and balanced the bike against the shop wall.

Although he could have slaked his thirst back home earlier with tap water, he had willed himself to hold out, to savour the moment when the sacred glass bottle was in his hand. The moment had arrived.

Before uncapping the Fanta, he pressed the freezing glass bottle to his burning forehead. Relief. He then unscrewed the top, tossed it to the ground, put the neck of the bottle to his lips, closed his eyes and tilted his head backwards, allowing the fizzy liquid to waterfall down his throat until it burned and some orange fizzled out through his nostrils. Happiness didn't come anymore pure and undiluted.

Charles's intention had been to return the change from the fiver to his mam's purse. His plan was stymied on two counts. The first had to do with his reasoning that his mother would recognise instantly that the fiver in her purse had turned into four one pound notes and loose change. The second obstacle was his mam's presence when he got home. He'd expected her to be still in bed. Despite her splitting headache, she was in the kitchen preparing his father's tea before he came home.

She confronted him about the missing money from her purse. Charles tried to deny it. But the thing is, mothers knew things. You couldn't lie to them. They possessed psychic powers. Another lesson he was introduced to that day.

He cried and said he was sorry. No use. She had already phoned his father in work. His father would talk to him later. Charles pleaded with her, but her head was thumping, she told him, and she didn't want to discuss it further.

When Charles heard his father's car pulling into the drive, he rushed upstairs and hid behind the freestanding wardrobe in his bedroom.

For a big man Charles's father could move with stealth, like a cat. He was in his room in minutes and knew exactly where Charles was hiding. He pulled out the wardrobe and spoke calmly, too calmly.

"Your tea is ready, son," he said. "C'mon, let's go."

No shouting or accusations. No threats or promises that he'd be going to bed early without comics on Friday night.

Charles trudged downstairs on front of his father, resisting easily the urge to slide down the banisters.

Besides his sister's manic tones, as she chirped on about herself and her friends, teatime in front of the telly had something odd about it. His father chewed his way through his poached eggs and toast, while his mam's eyes fastened to the salad and cottage cheese on her plate – part of her latest diet.

Only in hindsight would Charles remember the stronger tell-tale signs: The way his mam's eyes bounced from her plate to his father more than once; and his father, staring at the TV screen as though he wasn't watching it. But strangest of all was that neither his mam nor his dad insisted he finish his toasted cheese sandwiches.

Charles's appetite had been replaced by a mild nausea. In his cheeks was a heated sensation from too much sun. Maybe that's why they didn't make him finish his tea. They felt sorry for him because of his sunburn.

Charles helped his sister carry the dishes to the sink when they'd finished eating. Something he never did. He even helped to wash some of the dishes until the theme music to his dad's favourite comedy, *Get Smart, Agent 86*, pulled him back into the living room.

It was good to see his dad laughing, his big face bursting with delight, at Maxwell Smart's antics.

"That's so funny," his dad said a number of times at something Smart said or did, the complexion of his cheeks turning from red to puce.

Charles busied himself with his sketchbook during the programme, listening to Smart's nasally tones and occasionally glancing up from his charcoal sketch.

At some stage he heard his sister leaving through the front door in her usual manner, without saying goodbye to anyone. Charles got on with his artwork.

By the time the show was over, he had drawn the outline of a bird with a curved beak, but hadn't yet decided if it was an eagle or a parrot.

Charles's father stretched his arms and yawned, got out of his chair and went into the back garden. Charles engrossed himself in his sketch.

"Do you have to, Jack?" Charles heard his mam ask when his father returned through the side door into the kitchen.

"Never did me any harm, did it?" his father asked. He was breathless. "My old man swore by it."

Everything speeded up after that moment.

His father closed the living room door behind him.

"Right, you," he said to Charles. "Upstairs."

"No, Dad, please, Dad. I'm sorry. I swear to God. I'll never do it again."

Charles ran to the other side of the table. His father worked his way around the centre table, holding the newly-cut switch in his flabby hand as though he were herding cattle. "Come here, you, until I – C'mere, I said." And he sliced the air with the switch, making a whistling sound.

Charles felt giddy running around the table, his father moving after him, muttering and wagging the raised up switch. He thought he might cry but his cry sounded more like laughing. That his laugh had a wobble to it was funnier still. And then it happened. The action that was to change Charles's understanding of everything he had learned in his first decade of life. Or, rather, the action that was to undo all he understood, shattering, forever, any possibility of ever trusting his father, or anyone else, for that matter, throughout his lifetime.

The pain in his cheek was unlike anything Charles had ever experienced. Or was it the shock? Onetime, while burning plastic up in the fields, some of the melting plastic had dripped onto his fingers. The bubbling plastic ate into his flesh and Charles had screamed his way to the hospital on the bus. Now there was a greater inferno flaming in his sunburned cheek where his father had caught him across the table with his homemade switch.

Not yet fully conscious of what had happened, Charles felt his father's stubby fingers clutching him and dragging him upstairs by his collar. The sharp downward slice of the switch on the backs of Charles's fingers as he attempted to cling onto the banisters overrode the fire in his cheek.

"Agghh, Dad, leave us alone, will you?" he roared. "I

was thirsty is all… only meant to borrow the money… I didn't mean to—"

"You're a lying, thieving little bastard," his father said and threw Charles down on the landing floor.

Charles felt the switch catch him across the bare legs, his ass, his back and his arms before the stick snapped.

"Fuck it," his father said.

"I'm sorry, Dad. I'll be good from now on. I promise I will" But his father wasn't yet through with him.

Charles heard his father unbuckling his belt. He squirmed on his belly so he could look up at him. A mistake. The sole of his father's foot pressed him into the carpet.

"Stay down," he roared.

In hindsight, for Charles, this part of his ordeal matched for shock the first crack across his face. *Stay down* were the last words his father uttered in advance of raining down a plethora of blows using his leather belt on Charles's already beaten body.

Perhaps it would have been no less wrong if his father had carried out his attack on Charles when he had arrived home and removed him from behind the wardrobe. Yet there was something even more wrong about sitting and laughing your way through a TV programme and then assaulting your own son. Charles was too young to reason this at the time, but he felt it in his belly.

Worse still was a leather belt cutting into the backs of your knees without the alleviation of critical or conciliatory words. Absent was the *This'll hurt me more than it will you* lie. Or even if his father had continued with his rant about what a delinquent Charles was, it would have been, not normal but, less abnormal.

The heavy grunts and wheezing of an overweight man were the only sounds that came from his father as he beat

Charles until he seemed unable to continue. He was exhausted.

Two years were to tick away without Charles and his father speaking to each other. That changed when his father bought him a ten-foot fishing rod and a multiplier reel for his thirteenth birthday. A promise his dad had made him a few years back.

"Wow. Thanks, Dad. Do you want to go fishing from the pier on Saturday?" he asked, as though they had never stopped communicating for two long childhood years.

"No, son. You go ahead. There's a game on the box I want to see on Saturday. Some other time."

There never was another time.

Charles regarded the relationship between he and his father for the remainder of his teenage years as an unspoken stand-off. Neither of them had too much to say to the other; they never did any father-son things together; and he was often made to feel like his father would be a far happier man if Charles were to just disappear.

In a way, Charles did disappear. He became more insular, seldom left the house, and stayed in his room drawing and painting whenever *he* was around. Watching the younger kids playing in the streets, the streets he once played in, from his bedroom window sometimes made him feel unreal, an imaginary figure in someone else's head.

His father, too, drifted further from the family unit that never quite was. He retired early, confined himself to the basement, which doubled as a spare room with its own bathroom, lost interest in eating, and somehow survived on a diet of alcohol, books and listening to the radio. There he remained, a burden and an embarrassment.

Except for special occasions, Christmas or Easter, Charles's father seldom emerged. For Charles, seeing how his father had shed all his huge bulk was akin to looking at a nightmare reflection, a vision of how he, Charles, might appear in a concentration camp.

Equally disturbing were his father's comments. "You can't even get yourself a bird," he'd say to Charles. "Or don't you like girls?"

Charles's sister he left alone, but his mam had to endure similar sarcasm.

"Pass me the gravy, Penny," he'd say, pretending he was confusing her with one of his sisters. Charles's mam and his aunts Penny and Maggie never got on.

Keeping her head down, Charles's mam tried to ignore his taunts. After all, it was Christmas, or some other special occasion, she would argue to Charles later.

"Leave her alone," Charles would say.

"Oh, sorry. I mean Maggie. My mistake."

The only other times his father left the basement were when Charles or his sister brought home friends. And those were rare occasions.

He'd stumble upon them as they were coming from the bathroom and make a personal comment, usually an observation about their appearance.

Charles's wife, Cathy, was French. A small and compact girl, she was neither a conventional beauty nor a frump. Above her upper lip was the faintest trace of a moustache. She wore it with the grace and aplomb of her race. His father changed all that. His father changed everything. Everything.

The priest was finished. He lowered his head, raised his eyebrows over his black-rimmed spectacles, and nodded once at Charles.

Charles experienced his body as a detachment from who he was. He rose to his feet.

Dear Lord, what would he say? He glanced at the boys,

their tiny faces smiled up at him. This was a day they would recall in years to come – well, Tommy would – he couldn't let them down. He couldn't sully further their memory of a grandfather they hardly knew.

He squeezed by his two aunts seated next to them, stepped from the pew and made his way to the altar.

Standing at the pulpit, he allowed his eyes to sweep over the congregation – a frightening turnout; too many faces. The beating inside his chest reverberated in his temples, and his legs seemed as though they might give out. He paused, waiting to hear what he would say.

"In a way my father, our father," he corrected himself and smiled at his sister. His voice sounded more confident than he had expected it to be. "Jack to his sisters and friends, Grandad to Tommy and Jamie, was a private man, a misunderstood man." There was a slight catch in his throat. He cleared it with a short cough and continued. "But for Jack, our two beautiful boys, Tommy and Jamie, would never have existed." He paused in order to swallow and home in on words that threatened to elude him. He couldn't locate a connection, but continued. "In his younger days – and Penny and Maggie will attest to this – Dad, Jack, was a keen fisherman. He first took me fishing when I was the same age as Tommy. Sometimes we travelled by car to a river or a lake. But mostly we fished the coastline in springtime and summer."

He scanned the faces and alighted on a couple of individual ones. They seemed to know he was looking at them. Charles could tell. He swept his vision away. "Made me feel so important tramping down a pier next to Dad, the two of us with our serious fishing rods and big, green canvas bags. Catching a fish was less important than just being out there, side by side, baiting hooks, casting our lines, watching the floats bobbing on the rippled waters and waiting for that thrilling tingle to shoot through the line, into your finger, up your arm and into your body."

Charles twisted sideways and locked his eyes onto his father's coffin. "Thanks, Dad," he said. Looking back at the familiar faces in the congregation, he went on. "Dad often dreamed that one day he would take Tommy and Jamie fishing. He promised Tommy he would when he grew bigger. Well, I guess Time, that *Old Bald Cheater*, has done him out of his dream." Charles could feel he was getting to the nub of what he hadn't known he'd been trying to say.

His job now was to wrap it up. "But there's one thing Time never counted on: his father's son." Did that sound pretentious? "So, next week, when the boys and me go fishing to one of their grandad's favourite freshwater rivers, it'll be their first fishing trip. We'll take the same trails Dad and me took along the riverbank, watching out for the blue and red dragonflies hawking insects over the water."

Tommy was smiling, he could see, listening to his dad mentioning his name. "When we get hungry we'll build a small fire, the way Dad and me used to, in front of a huge boulder that's shaped like an elephant, and cook up our catch."

Moving only his eyes, Charles glanced sideways at his father's coffin. Okay, he had it. Closure. He inhaled a deep breath into his lungs. "More than anything that Dad taught me was to keep a promise. And together he and I are going to honour the commitment he made to Tommy and Jamie. The boys and me, along with their grandad, are going fishing this very day next week." Hesitant applause rippled from the back of the church, an incoming wave working up momentum, before crashing on the shore of the altar at Charles's feet.

There, he'd done it. His mam would have been proud of him.

Adios España, Adios

A baby boy died during my night shift on Friday. He was seventeen months old and had a smile so angelic, I could almost have begun to believe in God again; the way I did when I was a kid, before I had sense to realize there was no sense to anything.

The boy's condition was congenital – a hole in his heart. Nothing we could do, but we tried to do it anyway. I'd been on twenty-four-hour call, worked twenty-one hours, and stayed on for a total of thirty-three hours without uninterrupted sleep. I would've stayed awake forever if I'd been able to keep that child alive; but he was born to die. We'd known this when he was still in his mother's womb.

A dark-skinned beauty with despair in her eyes, the dead boy's mother cursed me in Catalan on the day of his birth. In charge of overseeing the delivery of the baby back then, I was the one to tell her of her child's destiny.

What a Christless world we live in. That's what was going through my mind on the short walk from the hospital to the railway station on Saturday morning. Christmas time. The shops displaying brightly coloured toys and pumping happy Christmas carols into the sun-filled street. Little children, saucer-eyed, pressing their palms to windowpanes, their piping voices blending with the Christmas music. Why him and not them? Why him and not me?

The sight of a street person wrapped-up in a sleeping bag, lying on a sheet of cardboard and wearing a beanie pulled down over his face, guarded by two sleeping dogs reminded me that I hadn't slept for a long time. The image of my waiting bed caused a sense of voluptuous longing to course sluggishly through me like oil. Then the truer image surfaced: being pickled in my own sweat, while I struggled to escape into sleep. The Spanish winter is mild, but my wife is always cold. She's had a timer placed on the heating system.

I didn't belong here anyway is what I thought when I boarded the train and took my seat. What was I, a Boston-boy and Harvard-graduate, doing in Jerez, Spain? A pretty Spanish girl in college, with a strange and endearingly crooked smile, dark brown eyes, and a perfect complexion was my reason for being here. But long hours and American drive pitted against a Latin temperament were combining to undermine our relationship way before we were married at the end of the summer.

Trying to stop myself thinking about Julia's pregnancy set the due date of the birth of our first child in tall, capitalized red letters in my head: *January 4th. Happy New Year.*

"For me is like a big joke," Julia says. "I'm married to a paediatrician who is never home for me, and my baby too when it arrives."

Julia has left our home to stay with her parents until the baby is born. We've agreed that this is better for both of us. Hopefully it's a way to patch up our failing marriage.

My focus of unhappiness had swung from the lifeless little corpse lying in the mortuary to my own marriage problems, when I spotted something black wedged down between the side of the railway carriage and the seat I was sitting in. I retrieved it easily: a wallet and quite heavy. Inside was a wad of fifty-euro notes, adding up to a few thousand at a glance. I stashed it self-consciously into my holdall.

Before collapsing into bed at home, I counted the money. Was this some kind of lousy joke on God's part? If I wasn't already asleep and dreaming, there was five thousand euro. What manner of god allows me to lose in a marathon battle to keep a child alive, then grants me a reward for losing?

Working shift hours has eroded my biological clock. And the muggy heat doesn't help. I slept badly and was awake by lunchtime. The wallet. The money. There it sat on the kitchen table as it had been in what I hadn't been sure were dreams.

While I recounted the cash, this time I experienced a bubbling sensation in my stomach, and my fingertips tingled. I was up to around twenty-five hundred when a triple knocking came from the front door. Pulling open the fridge, I threw in the wallet and stuffed the notes behind a bowl of something.

Through the frosted glass pane of the front door stood a dark figure wearing a hat. The police. They had me – but for what? I'm a professional, I told myself. A doctor, I rehearsed in an internal speech. A doctor who was fully intent on… No. I killed the idea. It felt contrived, too premediated.

I strolled to the door and drew in a deep breath of oxygen. I opened the door, keeping one hand on the handle and the other on the doorframe. A surgeon's hands weren't supposed to shake.

"Hola, señor." The postman. "Sign here, please, sir," he regurgitated automatically in English.

I signed the pad, accepted the registered letter, and thanked him.

Ensuring the postman had definitely gone, I started counting again from the first note. I made it through the second count without disturbance. I'd miscounted; well, miscounted because I overlooked a few five hundred euro notes in another compartment. Nine thousand was the new figure.

I caught sight of my reflection in the silver kettle, and saw a smile that didn't seem to belong to my face. It was only then that I looked properly at the identification card.

Javier Alberto Fernandez was the name below a striking photo of a deeply tanned guy with ink-black hair in his thirties, whose high and prominent cheekbones made him look more American Indian than Spanish.

Nobody carries around nine thousand in cash unless he makes his money outside the law, I told myself.

While fixing a large mug of black coffee, I went on a spending spree in my head. Back home everyone would be amazed at my financial success in Spain. And envious, too, which was more important.

I saw myself through the eyes of family members as they stood outside the barrier of the arrivals area in JFK airport. A dashing figure in a full-length Yves Saint Laurent cashmere coat emerges. Me. As we draw near to greet each other, the flashing lights of a nearby Christmas tree reflect in my eyes and complement my bronzed skin. At home, my little sister, Mandy, is inconsolable with delight when she opens a jewellery box and pulls out a small fortune in dollars. She always preferred gifts of cash, and I'd have no idea what to buy a fourteen-year-old girl anyway.

With these thoughts and images flashing in my head, I picked up the brown envelope and slit it open with the handle of my teaspoon. I slipped the letter free and felt an instant hot-coldness dampen my brow. It was from Mom. Something caught me by the throat. I could tell straight off that she'd written it while drinking or, at least, when not quite sober. She gets maudlin when she drinks. That didn't make the gushing sentiments any easier to take. I could picture her writing it while lying in bed, with the curtains still drawn late in the afternoon, a vague hum of stale urine and cheap wine in the airless room, her soft crying turning to that terrible wailing that terrified Mandy and I during the months after Dad first went into hospital.

In the letter Mom began by saying that I wasn't to

worry, and how much she loved me, more than she'd ever loved anybody. But in the same sentence said that life, for her, was no longer worth living. Since the day I'd left, she might as well have been put to sleep. What was her life for now that I, like our father, had deserted her? The days were without meaning. Everything she did was done for its own sake: eating, sleeping, getting out of bed, going to the grocers, and staring at the TV. She went on to say a few things that infused the empty longing that had gripped me with confused embarrassment. If it were possible, she would like if she and I could be the same person, able to feel, touch, smell and see the same things. Reading the words laid out like this on the page highlighted Mom's hearing disability; something that only ever became an issue for us growing up when other kids, in their inherent cruelty, made fun of the fact from time to time.

Reading on to the part where she suggested that she wished she could devour me, or be devoured by me, so that nothing could ever keep us apart, triggered such an unfocused rage in me, I cursed aloud at myself, and Mom too, and hammered my fist hard on the tabletop, spilling some coffee. I swabbed up the spilled coffee using part of the sports section ripped from yesterday's paper. I resisted the urge to crumple the letter or rip it to shreds. I read on. There was worse to come.

Mandy. Mandy was going all wrong. That's the way Mom put it. My heart quailed. There were boys and parties. Late nights. And sometimes she never came home at all. She was drinking, and worse, with her friends. She missed schooldays, and never studied anymore. Besides partying and cavorting with boys, the only other thing she seemed interested in anymore was playing tennis.

When Mom questioned her, Mandy went into hysterics, screaming and roaring that she had no right to judge her.

She'd called Mom some terrible names. A drunken old hag was the one that cut Mom up most. When she was at home, Mandy locked herself into her bedroom. She ignored Mom's pleas from outside the door, except to finally open it, if Mom persisted, so Mom could lip-read the foul language vomited into her face.

A roar exploded from my larynx. Shaking uncontrollably, I locked my palm to my mouth and listened for signs that the neighbours in the apartment above might have heard my outburst. The sound of daytime TV played on. Unable to control my shaking and the nerve beating at the side of my head, I felt myself succumbing to a solution I hadn't applied to myself for a long time.

I left the kitchen table and went into the spare room where I've been sleeping since Julia exiled me from our bedroom. I opened my kit and took out a scalpel. Careful to avoid an artery, I drew the blade quickly across my forearm. The instant stinging pain gave me the refocus I required. In the bathroom I dabbed the incision with a weakened solution of iodine before covering it with a bandage. I then returned to the kitchen and to Mom's letter.

To counter the throbbing nerve starting up again in my head, as I finished reading the last part of the letter, I worked my fingernails under the plaster and pressed them into my self-inflicted wound. Mom couldn't be sure who had started it, Mandy or her tennis coach. She couldn't be certain either of the extent of their involvement together. What she did know was that he, the coach, was twenty-eight, and that he'd been lately arriving outside the house in a black sports car it looked like. A convertible.

I dug my fingernails deep into the wound and worried my torn flesh. Why the hell did so much crap come all at once?

By the time I'd settled down a bit and swallowed the

last mouthful of bitter coffee, I was stabbing the digits of the phone number on the Spaniard's business card into my mobile phone. At least some of us were normal, law-abiding citizens. The money was tainted, unclean. Ten years of honest dedicated study, struggling in part-time jobs to cover rent and bills so I could remain in squalid flats and achieve my goal were sacrifices I wasn't going to flush away in a moment of avarice.

"Hello. Is that Javier Alberto Fernandez?" I asked.

"Who is this?" the voice on the end of the line answered.

"I have your wallet," I said. "I mean you are Señor Fernandez?"

We arranged to hook-up that afternoon, just the day before yesterday, Saturday, in a café near the railway station.

I arrived a half hour early to relax myself, but the long wait filled me with such agitation, I became a fidgeting, scratching, time-checking source of amusement for a few pretty Spanish teenage girls at a nearby table.

The girls lost interest in me and their attention was fully commandeered at exactly three-thirty p.m., as the hombre I was awaiting entered the café. Unlike his identification photo, he wore carefully sculpted facial hair. He sucked in his lower lip, on which clung a button-sized growth of hair. He had a moustache, too, an Errol Flynn-job. Thin, though toned in appearance, his clothes served to intensify his masculinity. He wore a stylish grey bomber jacket with a black shirt and expensive-looking dark slacks. He impressed, as might a bullfighter, conveying the cocky self-assuredness of someone accustomed to the constant adulation of women and the unswerving respect of men.

From the moment he shook my hand and sat down, he spoke to me in English, which was far better than my

Spanish. While we talked, he looked directly into my eyes without blinking. This unnerved me. He seemed fascinated with America and American politics.

"What do you think about the Vietnam War?" he asked, in a manner that suggested it had only recently taken place.

"I'm a doctor," I said, "and totally opposed to the wanton destruction of human life."

"No, please, señor, talk to me as a man, with feelings and emotions. I'm not a TV camera."

Suddenly this guy irritated me.

"Look, I don't wish to be impolite. You have your money. Now I've got to go." But he was a persuasive guy and, although my gut told me to be wary of him, he was an uncommon man, and I've never failed to be attracted by the singular.

The indefinable quality that gave me cause for caution brought to mind a couple of patients I've encountered over the years. The patients seemed normal when I first entered the ward, but suddenly lashed out with clawing fingernails or sunk their teeth into my hand. A concentrated, wild glint came into the eyes of these women before their attack. The bullfighter didn't display this characteristic, though he inspired the same feeling of apprehension in me.

George Bush was a terrorist, he ranted. Bush, like Saddam, should also go on trial for heinous crimes against humanity. Both of them, he stated as a fact, should be 'dispatched'. With fierce passion, he recalled an image he'd witnessed on a TV documentary about America's invasion of Vietnam. An American soldier held a knife to the throat of a Vietnamese child, while the terrified and helpless family of the distraught child looked on.

His description disturbed me. The innocent face of the angel-boy who had died under my blade the day before exploded into my thoughts. He, the infant-angel, had never known fear or hate, and he never would. A fuzzy thought. Was I attempting to convince myself that the consolation for early death lay in escaping the horrors of living?

There were too many conflicting thoughts in my head; I didn't know what I was supposed to think. That's when the bullfighter graduated to the Spanish government.

His brashness left him. He studied the other customers in the café carefully. When the waitress drew near, he stopped talking. When he did speak, he spoke in maddened whispers. He went into a confused and confusing diatribe against the Spanish government. To convince me to agree with his convictions seemed everything for him. I pigeonholed him into the category of a manic obsessive.

By now realizing that I must employ more tact with this individual, I told him I was on call, due back at the hospital, gave him a fictitious number and promised we'd hook up again in a couple of days. Placated, he rose as did I, took my extended hand and shook it vigorously. Without even having to look at the note he was pressing into my palm, I knew what he was doing. I'd refused his monetary offer as a reward three times during our one-sided conversation. He was already exiting the café and ignoring my protestations with a smile and a wave by the time I squeezed out from behind the corner table we'd been sharing.

I paid the bill, ignoring the cashier's attempt at humour in my efforts to catch the waitress's eye. I caught it, indicated that she leave what she was doing for a moment and come back to the counter. She needed little persuasion.

"Thank you, sir," she said. "Happy Christmas."

I smiled a forced smile and stepped into the street. Nearby, the bum with the beanie sat cross-legged at his patch outside the railway station. With his back pressed against a streetlamp, a pensive expression on his dignified face, and flanked by his two dogs, a hairy mongrel and a well-groomed Lassie collie, he possessed a ragged nobility.

The fallen king looked at the money I placed in his dog bowl before acknowledging me. He bowed his head slightly in my direction, thanked me and wished me a happy holiday through a controlled expression, then picked up the notes and coins without counting them – five-hundred-euro less the price of a cappuccino, an American coffee and the waitress's tip – and tucked them into his shirt pocket.

I'd almost managed to delete the meeting with the bullfighter from my mind later that evening. Crowding my imagination were thoughts of a snow-covered Harvard campus, seeing my little sister again and, hopefully, sorting her out, and helping Mom with the Christmas tree, driving her places in a rental car, and telling her everything, the way I always did. Mom is the only one who really understands me. She's the one who persuaded me to come to Spain to be with Julia. Dad was still alive but dying when I left three years ago. Leaving felt like such an act of betrayal, but when I didn't return for Dad's funeral, I knew I was damned.

I've been home once since then, and Mom convinced me to drop all charges against myself. Without wishing to sound like a premediated Oedipus, I wish I'd met my mom before my dad met her.

I was half dozing in a hot bath and listening to heavy rock music blasting from the stereo in the front room, when my mobile rang. Now I can shut down and relax to Jimi Hendrix's *Voodoo Chil*e, but whenever my mobile sounds, I come to life with the alertness of an animal whose survival depends upon senses sharp as a scalpel.

I pulled myself from the bath, cursing aloud, and padded on the balls of my feet into the front room and answered the phone.

"Hey amigo," the voice replied.

"How did you get my number?" I asked, remembering halfway through the sentence that I'd given it to him – but I'd given him a fictitious number.

"Hey, it's cool, man, as you say in America. You called me from your mobile originally, remember?"

I felt embarrassed now, and was sort of conscious, too, of the possible damage the suds from my ear and hands might be having on the mobile.

"Anyway," he went on. "You're a nice guy. I want to help you."

"I don't want any more of your money. You already—"

"Forget money, amigo. This is bigger than money. Are you going home for Christmas?"

"Listen, man. I'm on call. I—"

"You finished your shift this morning, Dave. You're back on duty tomorrow at seven a.m."

Taken aback at his knowledge about my affairs, I allowed a short silence to ensue.

"What do you want?" I asked.

"Listen to me. I happen to know that you are going home for Christmas. What I don't know is the exact date."

"Now you get this, my friend. I don't—"

"Be quiet, Doctor. Please."

His tone had the weight of authority – a man who must be listened to. I listened.

"I want to warn you," he continued. "Let's call it advice. Call your family, David, and tell them that your Christmas leave has been cancelled. You don't want to be on a plane over the holiday period."

"Are you telling me that?"

"Stay away from the airport, Doc. At least until the New Year."

That's when he put the phone down. I've tried to call

his number dozens of times since then, but a recorded message bleats out that it doesn't exist.

I haven't experienced the sense of frustrated anger that's gripped me over the last forty-eight hours since I was a boy and my dad became wheelchair bound through a rare paralysing illness. Dad is the reason I devoted my life to medicine. I hated him at first for leaving Mom, Mandy and me. There he was spending all his days in a hospital bed with tubes and wires sticking into his dead body. Only his eyes moved. My sister and I whimpered and cried with the stinging cold, while we held Mom's hands and trudged through the winter nights to catch the bus to visit Dad in hospital. And every time we got back home, I was so aware of our big, black car – another invalid – sitting mockingly in the driveway. Mom was always going to learn to drive. She never did. She was too nervous.

My adult years have been wholly taken up with bringing life into the world. But there have been moments, quite lucid and rational, throughout the past two days when it seemed pure reason that whoever is responsible for my almost being stranded in Spain for Christmas should die.

Less rational, I admit, is my suspicion about the postman. Our paths crossed again this morning as I returned to the house with freshly baked bread. He handed me a few Christmas cards from the folks back home and made a quip about anthrax. My body stiffened, and psychotic notions that nonetheless seemed sane seized me. He clearly recognized something odd in my countenance, and took off at the speed of one of his more classical predecessors.

The plane on which I'm a legal captive has been airborne for nearly five hours now. I've eaten nothing since breakfast. If they've laced the in-flight food with something to knock out the passengers, I'm the only one who'll be awake to pervert their twisted plan.

I need to go to the toilet, but that'll wait. There are a couple of Arabic-looking guys upfront who probably know who I am. These guys are all connected. If one of them decides to approach me in my seat, he'll be surprised to feel the tip of the gold pen with which I'm writing this being rammed into his chest. I'll stab him a few times to make sure I get the coronary arteries. And, if I can, I'll also thrust it lower down, aiming to puncture his kidneys and lungs.

But if, however, my bullfighting friend turns out to be a crank of sorts, I'll regard it as a duty to return to Spain, track him down, administer a lethal injection into his system and watch him wilt.

The world has no place for misguided fools. No more than it has for predators who prey on fourteen-year-old girls – destroyers of the innocent. Baby killers. An injection is too humane for the latter pariah. A tentative laceration drawn across his windpipe is the only solution, so that he may bleed away his existence, his astonished eyes burning into mine, fully aware and coming to terms with his unacceptable and heinous crime against the innocent.

The Panicked Rat

Christmas Eve: cold and sparkling. Happy faces. Children's voices, like chirping birds, twittering about Santa. And the shoppers smiling and simpering their apologies for getting in each other's way.

Patrick avoided eye contact with the passers-by. Yet he could feel their sneering eyes boring into him. They knew, the bastards.

The twenty-minute walk to the car park was one Patrick had made twice a day, weekdays, for seventeen years. His feet were familiar with every pavement crack, kerbstone height, and road width on the route.

How could everything continue in such a normal fashion, as though everything was the way it had always been? What would he tell Jenny? And Elliot? The panicked rat behind Patrick's eyes, the one whose familiar gnawing he'd somehow managed to contain when the Chief Executive told him, smilingly, that the company was putting his services on hold, squealed, chewed and tore at the inside of his head.

Jingly-jangly Christmas music jeered at Patrick through the bazaar's open shop-front. Coloured and sparkling lights drew his reluctant eyes into the shop. A blast of perfumed heat clawed at his face. Nauseated, he walked on, his every footfall detonating a thunderbolt that scourged the already tormented rat.

The tinny sound of the *William Tell Overture* blasting through his earpiece impacted on Patrick like one pain superseding another. He tore the cell phone from his inside jacket pocket and flipped it open. Jenny's name throbbed accusingly on the orange screen. He squeezed down the 'off' button, the way he might crush a loathsome bug, before replacing it in his pocket. He needed time to think, to get the words right.

Finances weren't the issue, not for a while anyway. There were the stocks, and the properties – although heavy mortgage repayments on one of the houses depended on regular income. The rent from the others paid for themselves.

As soon as Patrick got the figures down on paper, worked out where to nip and tuck – a favourite expression of Jenny's – he'd get on to her and explain everything.

Drawn by a bunch of carol singers down a side lane, he was beginning to feel a kind of perverse delight at the prospect of being a free man, owing allegiance to nobody other than his family. Maybe good would come out of it all. He'd have more time to spend with Elliot, and the baby would stop making strange noises when Patrick came into the room.

Through a large window above the singers, a softly-lit café, one Patrick had never noticed, shimmered with silhouetted figures. A lust to be among those figures strove to override his expanding feeling of bloated panic. He went inside.

Christmassy. The café felt Christmassy. That's how Jenny had described the city when they'd gone shopping over the weekend. "Everything's so Christmassy," she'd said. She was like a big kid at this time of year.

For what seemed maybe five minutes, Patrick wandered around the floor hoping to beat the other stragglers to a table being vacated. Finally he settled to sit with a gaunt-faced man who wore his straight grey hair in a ponytail.

Two slurps into his coffee, the man spoke to him as though they were friends and were already deep into a topic of conversation that fascinated them both. "Have you ever had any spiritual experiences yourself?" he asked. His voice was heavy accented and his words were encased in the gauche jauntiness of a man deluded of his own worth.

Patrick heard himself leaving too long a gap in answering this stranger, and mumbled something about having an appointment.

"The first time She appeared to me I was in the Joy," the man went on. "You know, Mountjoy prison?" A dirty brown line ran midway along his upper teeth.

"I think maybe you've got me confused with someone," Patrick said.

The man leaned forward over the table and whispered, "You see, I was a bad boy in me younger days." His breath smelled like some dead thing, recently discovered, that had ended over a week ago.

"If you don't mind," Patrick said. "I've had a not so great day." He needed another coffee.

The man shook with a low wheezy chuckle that put Patrick in mind of a TV puppet. "There's nothing to worry about, brother," he said, and stretched out his arms, palms up. The undersides of his fingers were yellow and shiny. "Everything's cool," he went on. "There's nothing that can't be sorted out if you give your number one vote to the Big Man." He dropped his head backwards and looked at the café ceiling.

"Look," Patrick said, "You'll really have to excuse me—"

"Women," the man said.

Twitching whiskers at the back of Patrick's eyes distorted his vision. He slumped back in his seat and massaged his temples. "I have to call my wife."

"Now don't get me wrong, brother. I never done nothing I shouldn't have done. I just love women is all. Our Lady didn't pull me up on that."

"Right," Patrick said, finally catching the attention of an androgynous-looking waiter that turned out to be a waitress. He asked for a café latte. She tapped the order into an electronic pad, turned to the man and blinked. He asked for a hot chocolate.

Patrick considered pointing out that they weren't together, but let it go. He'd be getting the tab. Nothing new there.

Patrick focused on the waitress disappearing into the heat and din. He sought refuge in his cell phone. Eleven missed calls – a text message informed him – and three voice messages. He dialled playback and listened. Jenny's recorded voice was difficult to hear above the café noise, and the signal wavered. She was in one of her moods. Hysterical. Drunk probably. He gleaned the gist of her message. What kind of a husband was he? Elliot and the baby may as well not have a father. And she hadn't been out anywhere for ages. The usual crap. He stabbed the cancel button, held down the 'off' key, and then snapped the phone shut. His hearing, despite itself, readjusted to the ramblings of the man opposite him.

The man's point was that women were expensive. Always crying out for this and for that. What could a decent worker do? He had to get the readies somehow.

"The way I see it is that opportunity exists so that we can use it," the man said. Aroused from its torpor in Patrick's head, the small furry thing with sharp teeth shuddered. "Working for a builder's suppliers, I was at the time," the man went on. "What started out as a mistake – I overfilled an order, and the customer looked after me, on the q.t., like – became a kind of sideline for meself."

"Why are you telling me this?" Patrick asked.

The other, stifling a yawn, stretched one arm behind his head and the other away from his side, brushing off the coat of an old woman leaving her table, and said, "Not a secret, brother. Everyone who knows me, knows me background."

Resisting the satisfying urge to tell this guy that he, Patrick, didn't know him, nor did he want to know him, he heard himself confessing how he may have lost his job for good that very day for burying figures where nobody should have ever found them. "I guess I got a bit too hungry." He stopped himself from mentioning the other issue in the office, how the female staff had conspired to allege how they had endured constant harassment from him since he took over as G.M.

"Ah, you and me is the same, brother." He extended his hand over the empty mugs at Patrick.

Cornered, Patrick felt, more than thought, that accepting this character's hand would be an admission of something hazy but ominous; akin to being forced to voice a confession for a crime of which you were innocent. The very act of speaking the words and formulating sentences that professed self-guilt gave legitimacy to untruths. A handshake was an even stronger distortion of truth.

"This is out of action since yesterday," Patrick said, holding up his right hand in a frozen claw-shape. "Snagged it, or, I mean, trapped it under a slab, you know, a patio stone in the front garden."

The man's bunched-up features drew closer to Patrick's hand, scrutinising it through pinprick eyes. "Oh right," he said, his head bobbing. "I get you."

A long naked tail, seedy-pink, shifted in and around Patrick's thoughts. Disgust and anger battled for supremacy within him. Why was he even bothering to explain himself to this guy? A guy who probably didn't even own a car, who surely lived in rented property, and had never known the awesome feeling of power at having control over a company's millions on the end of his fingertips.

"Listen, it's been very interesting talking to you, brother," Patrick said. He'd never called anyone 'brother' in his life. "The refreshment's on me," he added, working his wallet free from his inside pocket.

"No, no. This is my throw, sir." He was already on his feet and had passed a note to the waitress and told her to keep the change before Patrick could protest.

"Well, that's very decent of you," Patrick said.

"Not a bother. It's nice to be nice."

Patrick accepted the man's extended hand, but only managed to almost grip the other's long shiny fingers. His new friend used his other hand to cup Patrick under the elbow and kind of slid his hand up Patrick's forearm to his wrist. Tiny feet scampered down Patrick's back as the man slinked around tables and towards the exit. Patrick tried to summon a feeling of guilt. The man who had just departed was a genuinely good guy. But the rippling feeling under his skin, caused by the clammy non-handshake, wouldn't go away.

Five minutes. That would be time enough to ensure he wouldn't bump into the man outside in the street.

He pulled up his shirtsleeve. The hairs where his Rolex had been were flattened and his smooth skin caught the café's lighting. It was just like the skin on those shiny fingers. He jerked his sleeve up to his elbow. "My watch. He took my watch."

Aware of the other customers watching him as he raced for the exit, he heard himself bleating the apology that he'd just been robbed.

Out in the brightly lit street it felt as though he were watching someone else running around, avoiding the threatened-looking and threatening faces that spat incoherent words at him, or others that laughed at him. Which way to run, left or right? The crowds seemed to be expanding. No escape – if he could only see above them.

A rubbish bin. He could get a greater view down the street if he stood on the bin.

The cold steel of the bin bit into his knee and it was

difficult to get a proper foothold in the bin's mouth. Raising himself off the ground, he felt his trouser leg catch and tear before he lost balance. He hit the pavement with a hard thump. He cried out in an intolerable pain he hadn't experienced since he was a boy. He lay there unable to move, one of his arms caught behind his own back.

Enclosed in a circle of bodies looking down on him, Patrick tried to see beyond them. Somebody started up with a good impression of Shane McGowan: '*It was Christmas Eve, babe, in the drunk tank...*'

Coloured lights hung across the street, too bright to make out the sky and see the stars. Above the lights the buildings they were attached-to loomed closer, pressing him, crushing him farther into the ground. Through the numbing screen of pain and the babble of the crowd, he could make out the faint howling of an ambulance siren. He allowed his eyes to close. Nowhere left to run. Trapped.

Gods and Ants

Standing on the harbour quay, Alfred saw how he could get the temporarily blinding effect of the evening sun spilling across the water's surface. Dispensing with preliminary sketches, he pencilled the outline of the harbour and its berthed fishing boats onto the canvas, which he had fastened to the wooden easel. Squeezing colourful blobs of paint in an ordered array around the kidney-shaped palette, his inner vision was already framing the finished painting.

The Parisians and visiting art connoisseurs encountering the painting during Alfred P. Parkinson's first major art exhibition, which would one day be staged in Sacre Coeur, would experience the scene's essence. He saw them marvelling at the paradise island blue sky and the more sombre blue reflecting in the sea below into which the overwhelmed sun bled white-gold.

On their tongues the coastal-air saltiness blends with the plaintive sound of the gulls screaming their interminable plea before the endless sea.

And the boats – patient, rusting leviathans, whose white, multi-eyed cabins have witnessed countless fishing adventures far out in the cormorant-black sea, watched over by a yellow moon, hours before the dawn spills across the horizon. The painting bids them draw near. No, nearer still. There. Close your eyes. Tighter. Now draw in through your nose the salty, fishy, fuel-mingling, no-nonsense reek. It's the smell the fisherman smells, but he no longer smells it, as he no longer feels the cold. He, the fisherman, is a rough, capable, self-contained man, as much a part of the sea as the razor-shell winter mornings and the toiling boats.

Open your eyes. See again the boats and listen to them creak and groan. Reach out – you can almost touch the remorseful murmurings made by these floating, ancient giants who have ferried hardy fishermen to their deaths.

The few aimless evening strollers who had gathered tentatively around Alfred and his easel pulled in others. They swarmed about him like ants crawling over a fallen raptor, flightless, though not yet dead. Their presence and proximity interfered with his concentration. Time and discipline was his defence – Gods were not peeved by ants.

"I'm telling you," Alfred overheard someone in the crowd remark. "The colour, the blue. He's got the blue wrong."

Alfred studied the blue pigment he had mixed and smeared across the upper and lower parts of his canvas using his palette knife. Should he have applied more white? His sky was a darker hue than that of the painting in his head. Trying to ignore the bodies around him and their increasing babble, he squinted upwards at the altocumulus clouds that were drifting ominously towards the spreading sun.

"Are you a painter, mister?" a small boy asked him, pulling at the side of his jacket. "Are you, mister?"

"I like painting," Alfred said. "What about you?"

The boy giggled through the mesh of his splayed fingers.

Mister, the kid had called him. Did he look like a mister? Like his father?

"Leave the man alone, Dwayne," a man's voice said, a daddy's voice.

"Sorry, bud," a younger guy, who'd been scrutinising his picture, said to Alfred. "And I'm sorry for asking you."

Alfred waited. The young man, whose prominent nose was peppered with blackheads, looked from the painting to the scene it represented and back to Alfred. His dull, unblinking eyes locked onto Alfred's.

"So," Alfred asked, "what do you want?"

The set expression on the young man's face was the stupid, animal confidence worn by a creature perpetually undaunted because it lacks the terms of reference to know any better.

"Ah, don't be like that," he said. "Now, I'm only asking, mind." He fired a quick glance at the harbour. "Do you see that boat there?" He aimed an index finger beyond a cluster of people and into the water. "The red and white one? It's got rust all over the shop."

"What about it?" Alfred said.

"Well, there's five roundy windows in the box part."

"The cabin, you moron," one of his mates corrected him.

"Now in your picture," he went on, "there's only four. Look it." And he counted them.

"That's because in this picture," Alfred said, "there are just four men on the boat. They don't need an extra window."

The gently mocking laughter of the people gathered nearest them made the young man look unsure. Maybe he was realising that his attempt at ridicule had somehow backfired.

"On your bike," someone shouted after the young man who was sprinting after his three pals on his stunt bike. His mates cursed and jeered him as they rocketed away, all of them on these stubby bikes looking like men who imagined they were boys.

Going through the motions of tidying up, cleaning his brushes and knife with a rag soaked in turpentine was Alfred's way of letting the crowd know that the show was over. They dispersed. Some towards their cars, while others filed across the path and out along the pier, a perfect spot from which to demystify the magic of the setting sun by gawping communally at the horizon.

Alfred's unfinished painting was no masterpiece. Masterpieces were limited. His flawed work was far superior to perfection. Once perfection was attained, there was nowhere left to go. Genius lay in conception and the striving towards an original dream.

Leaving the canvas perched on the easel, he reversed away from it until the departing light dulled its colours and weakened its forms. Behind and surrounding his presumptuous dabbling, the day's fiery symphony reached its skin-tingling crescendo, clutching Alfred by the throat, its cool, slender fingers bringing him to submission. As though in genuflection, he collapsed to one knee. The phantom fingers released his windpipe and ran their crimson claws along his bare arms, burrowed beneath his T-shirt and tore lustfully at his torso. Even the nearby canvas shuddered at the evening's touch.

A squeaking sound coming from the plastic crates filled with dead crabs a few feet away made him more aware of the fetid hum of overripe fish. A crab moved. The creature was alive. A survivor. Alfred would grant the crab its deserved freedom. Maybe there were others, too.

An oily, black-furred creature popped up from beneath the solid crab carcasses. A rat. It seemed to look Alfred full in the face before pulling itself free of the crate and kind of stumbling when it hit the ground. Scuttling away, it dragged an unseemly, long pink tail with it.

Alfred felt nauseated and sidled away from the fish stench. The wind shifted, and the sickening stink followed him.

Probably it was the same serpentine streak of wind that tentatively prodded his canvas, which clattered like a boat's sail, before toppling. The easel and canvas appeared to swoon face-forward in slow motion, flip sideways, clip the lip of the quay, and slide resignedly over the edge.

The gratifying splash as it slapped the water's surface pierced the evening's swelling contentment, the way a rifle report punctuates a perfect morning.

"Christ I'm shattered," she said. "Can you not come to bed? One of us has to get up in the morning."

"Keep it down, will you?" he said, turning from the curtain. "He'll hear you."

Millie flipped over her pillow, slapped it hard, and twisted around to face the wall.

From where he positioned himself at the side of the net curtain, peering into the front garden, the high golden privet hedging made it difficult to see the pavement.

Hugh and Millie had been caught out twice already this month. The first time they'd discovered a plastic sack of rubbish left with theirs the night before refuse collection, and on the second occasion the night-time prowlers had deposited three sacks. Hugh took the sacks in and opened them on the front lawn. He could find nothing incriminatory – no headed letters or bills – nothing that would stand up as categorical proof that their next-door neighbours were offloading their household rubbish on them. But Hugh knew. Who else could it be?

As the current working-from-home partner in their marriage, the rubbish thing was interfering with his work. Half drawn-up plans that should have been almost completed by now on a project he'd been working on since Christmas looked much the same to Millie for weeks whenever she glanced at them in the box room masquerading as Hugh's temporary office. A heated sensation, originating in Hugh's neck and rising instantly into his face, engulfed him when she put her observation to him a few days ago.

"Strawberry Crisp," he replied.

"Sorry?" she said.

"The stuff with the dried strawberries and the cluster yokes."

"What are you talking about?"

"They have it for breakfast."

Hugh heard himself prattle on about how he came across the Strawberry Crisp carton in one of the three bags he'd scoured through on the lawn, and had that very day seen the same cereal packet nestling in Yvette's shopping trolley.

"You followed her to Tesco's?" she asked.

"I needed a few things."

"We got the groceries on Thursday."

Now he was sorry he'd told her. What he didn't tell her was that he'd also been keeping notes on Dermot and Yvette's movements. Even took a few pictures. Everything was coming together.

For Hugh, Dermot was the sucked-in innocent in all of this. A regular nine-to-five office worker with the National Telephone Company, Dermot was as inoffensive and predictable as a grazing bullock. Always a cheery smile and a fulsome "Hello, Hugh. And how's the man?" Hugh had lately detected a significant alteration in Dermot's manner since the onset of this clandestine business with the rubbish.

Hugh made a point on one of the evenings of being in the front garden around the time Dermot got in. Dermot remained in his car, supposedly tinkering with something, and then, as soon as Hugh hunkered down into the flowerbed, he heard Dermot's car door clicking open and slamming shut. By the time Hugh raised himself to his feet, Dermot's back was disappearing around the corner of the house for the side entrance.

Yvette was behind it all. He'd never taken to her. Yvette with her condescending "Hello there," always after a second's delay, as if Hugh's intrusive presence, his very being, was something she had to endure, the way she had to accept mud after rainfall.

Yvette had the sort of sneaky face Hugh detested. When not gabbing on at Millie across the garden fence, Yvette's thin-lipped mouth was puckered into affected interest, the crimson lipstick painted outside the rim of her lips giving the disturbing impression of an unfortunate injury.

"Millie," Hugh whispered and drew back from the window.

Millie's clogged voice mumbled in her sleep.

"Wake up, Millie. Millie I see something."

The something, a fox, cleared the gap in the hedge and into the street. Before skittering off into the night on spindly legs, the creature turned its head over its shoulder and seemed to look directly up at Hugh who watched it from behind half-closed blinds. In the faraway blackness of the night, he heard the fox's bark, clear and cold, a sound so eerie as to confound a non-believer from his rigid stance.

"What's he doing?" Millie asked. "Can you see?"

"Nothing," Hugh said. "It's just a fox. Go back to sleep."

That's when Millie announced she wasn't going to be able to take much more of this. The usual ranting came next. Hugh said he was sorry. Pointless. Millie banged on, told him to leave her alone. Hugh said he'd go into the spare room, give her some space, so she could sleep properly.

"Good," she said.

Later on, Millie's anxious voice dragged Hugh from sleep in the spare room, though he thought he'd been lying there awake for hours.

"It's her," she said. "It's Yvette, not Dermot. I saw her going back inside in her nightgown."

Millie persuaded Hugh to leave it till the morning. They could check the rubbish before he dropped her down to the train station.

Back in their double bed together, Millie, wide awake

now, declared that she was willing to take partial blame for her and Hugh not being 'too friendly' with each other of late. She snuggled into Hugh's back and slid her lips around his neck.

Hugh tensed up. He told her he hadn't felt so bushwhacked in ages.

"Bushwhacked," Millie repeated and let her hand slide down from his chest and onto his belly. "Mmmmmm."

"I mean it, Millie," he said, sitting up. "I'm way behind on the drawings and plans. I need to sleep."

It was Millie's turn to abandon their bed. She ignored his pleas to return. He watched her silhouette fumble in the quarter-light for her clothes, the wire hangers clashing and crashing in the wardrobe spoke for her. She pulled the bedroom door shut behind her with too much force. Hugh's heavy eyelids closed.

"I'm late now," Millie's voice said, bludgeoning him from sleep. "I thought you were up?"

The morning struck him like an unexpected blow to the solar plexus. He raised himself onto his elbow, then pushed himself from the bed and, standing, began to drag on his clothes.

"Forget it," she said. "I'll be quicker now if I run." And she was gone out the door.

Hugh made no attempt to follow her. As soon as he was spruced up – an operation that lasted an hour and fifteen minutes – Hugh padded out to the bin in his flip-flops.

There it was, deposited like a cuckoo's egg on top of their rubbish in the opened black bin, the same plastic green bag as the last time. A staccato rhythm beat a steady tattoo at the side of Hugh's head. He nodded up at Yvette's window, affected a knowing smile, held out the green bag by the scruff of the neck, the way a magician might dangle a white rabbit for an incredulous audience, pointedly looked at the bag and back up at the window, and then carried it at arm's length into the garden to the front lawn.

The usual household crap: soiled kitchen towels, slimy bean tins, weeping fruit rinds and mushy vegetable trimmings. Very clever. Hugh had been waiting to alight upon the cereal packet, the definitive and damning evidence.

But this time there was no Strawberry Crisp; the piece of evidence on which his case rested.

But wait. There was something else: a small white bag, tightly and self-consciously knotted. Using the serrated kitchen knife with which he'd opened the green bag on the lawn, Hugh punctured the white bag and ripped into it. Then, mantling it with his body, his back to Yvette's window, he picked up the bag and pulled the item of underclothing free, his fingertips working the material as though its texture might impart some great truth. He was positive he'd seen the same type hanging out to dry on Yvette's clothesline.

Enclosing the silky pink material in his fist, Hugh took it to the back garden where he put it into an empty flowerpot in the garden shed. Before returning to the house, he closed the shed door behind him, retreated to the shed's darkest corner behind the lawnmower, the flowerpot pressed to his chest, scooped up its silky contents, pressed it to his face and inhaled deeply.

Unsure how he might broach the delicate issue, the damning evidence, Hugh gave Yvette a good three-quarters of an hour before calling to her door after he'd observed her, glistening with sweat and grey track suited, returning home.

About to walk away when his third attempt at rapping on the front door glass went unanswered, the upstairs window opened.

"Oh, Hugh," Yvette said, hanging out the window. "Give me a tick. I'm just out of the shower." Around her head was a white towel, and what appeared to be a beach towel with a dolphin motif which she held in place around her body.

Surprisingly, Yvette came to the door immediately, clothed in the towels. In the living room she told him to relax and to just make himself right at home. He'd have a cuppa of course, and without waiting for his reply she was in the kitchen and filling up the kettle. It was as though she'd been expecting him.

"There we go," she said, sitting down so close to him, he could feel the moist heat radiating from her towel-covered body. "I was wondering when we'd finally get together."

"Sorry?" he said, unconsciously shifting a few inches away from her on the sofa.

"Oh, come on. I've seen you watching me." She removed the towel from her head in a twist and swung her hair free, its wet ends striking him lightly in the face. She smelled like clematis in springtime.

"No, no. You've got me wrong. I wasn't. I was—" He found no explanation to grab onto. He drew his hand across his damp brow, and then crossed his wrists over his lap. Why hadn't he put on a pair of jeans?

"What do you do when you spy on me from that window of yours when Millie's at work?" Her voice was smiling and she playfully followed his retreating eyes with her whole face. The kettle in the kitchen began to hiss loudly.

"I don't. Look. I better… I've got to…" he tried to push off the sofa, but Yvette's fleshy thigh swinging over his lap stopped him from rising. Unbelievably she squirmed into his lap, facing him, and removed the dolphin-themed towel, which fell to the floor behind her like a discarded cloak.

Was this really happening?

"Millie told me about your little," she paused, "shall we say, *problem*."

"What?" he said. The import of Millie's impossible act of betrayal seeped into the confused moment and stirred in him anger. The hissing kettle was now whistling. "Get off me, Yvette. Can you please… What if Dermot… Please."

"What's this?" she said. Her eyes left his and peeked over her own swollen breasts between them. With her eyes fastened to his again, she took him in her hand and guided him. He slipped in easily. She then began to move in his lap, the corner of her lower lip clamped in her teeth.

And then it happened. The switch that had for so long remained untouched was flicked. Yvette's cutting eyes closed as she locked her mouth to his. He felt his tongue and mouth sucking, licking and biting accordingly.

Banished now were any lingering thoughts of righteousness over offloaded rubbish bags, as were the images of stinking, decaying matter with its bleeding, oozing and festering wounds. In their place the flicked switch cast a light so white it burned within him, below him and on him, as Yvette rocked him towards what was now unstoppable, inevitable, her damp, hot skin pungent and pure, as the screaming kettle reached its crescendo, a long, drawn-out note more mysterious, more divine than the bark of a city fox prowling its urban territory on a sultry summer's night.

Van Gogh's Ear

Another birthday. My thirty-seventh. Somehow there seemed great significance attached to my being thirty-seven. There were famous figures in history who didn't quite kick off their careers till they were thirty-seven. George Bernard Shaw was one of them; that I knew. And there were others too, but I couldn't think of any. I'd do a Google on them later.

The connection with great men, tentative though it was, had me humming and half-singing to myself in the bathroom. Good acoustics!

The wave of excitement sloshing about in my stomach, as I shaved in front of the bathroom mirror, set off minor shockwaves that worked their way up my arm and into my hand, which trembled and caused me to nick my jawbone. The flesh wound was deeper than I at first imagined, so I pressed a tiny piece of toilet paper against the cut to stem the bleeding. That's what my dad used to do.

Cleaned up and refreshed, I treated myself to three slices of French toast with fried eggs and sausages before I could get myself down to work. The occasional unhealthy fry-up couldn't, surely, affect my high cholesterol. Besides, Bruno ate his usual share of my breakfast.

Bruno, my five-year old Pyrenean Mountain Dog, recognizes an unwritten rule in our house: half of everything on a plate set before me is his entitlement. Lately, since I jacked-in my job last month, Bruno's had more opportunity to exercise his rights. When Margaret's home from work, she insists I put Bruno into the backyard. Margaret can't stomach the stringy saliva that hangs from Bruno's muzzle and clings to his fur while the dog begs and we eat. She says too that Emer might catch something from him.

My mobile rang just as I was shoving the dirty plates into the already cluttered sink. The ring-tone, the latest one I'd downloaded, *Ride of the Valkyries*, ignited miniature fireworks in my stomach.

Someone calling to wish me Happy Birthday, I guessed as I fumbled to get the phone from its leather case. Maybe not. The name throbbing on the screen – Tony's Security Company – told me otherwise. I let it ring another couple of times. Didn't want to appear too anxious, or have him think I'd nothing better to do on my birthday than take phone calls.

"Hello."

"Eight o'clock tonight," Tony's heavy voice said. That was it. No 'Hey Ray, Happy Birthday, man'. Not even a simple 'How's things, man?'

"Listen, Tony. Today's my birthday." I left a pause. Silence. "You know I don't like letting you down—"

"Look," he interrupted. "You want the hours or not? I've plenty other chaps on me books."

"Sure," I heard myself saying in a cheery tone that wouldn't have fooled even me. "Can do. So that's eight till closing time, is it?"

"Double shift," he said. "I need a man to stay on and work the club as well."

I accepted. Fuck me, I accepted.

"Shit," I shouted, as I snapped the phone shut.

Bruno yelped. His offended look pierced me.

"No, not you, boy. Come here, Bruno. That's a good lad."

Bruno slobbered, licked and chewed gently around my fingers and hands, his doleful eyes locked to mine.

My earlier plan to get down to a bit of work I put on hold. The more pressing need now was to convince Bruno my bad mood had nothing to do with him. And why did I have to have an excuse not to work anyway? After all, it was my birthday, wasn't it?

The way Bruno whined and bounded about like a giant puppy, because we were going for a ramble at the wrong time of day, injected me with a dart of sunshine. Sure I needn't worry about the double-shift later, I told myself. I wasn't due on the door of the hotel till eight, the club opened at eleven and we'd be closing-up shop by two-thirty. By three-fifteen I'd be on the way home, and by dawn I'd have slipped into bed next to Margaret's warm body.

I decided to take Bruno on foot to the walkway along the nearby canal bank. That way I'd waste less time driving to the park, a good seven kilometres away, and would be back with time to spare before Margaret popped home for lunch. I might, after all, get some work done, even though it was my birthday.

Once we'd left the busy roads and the anxious pavements, there were few people knocking about along the canal bank. Those I did pass made me feel guilty about sauntering through the morning, while everyone else was clicked into work-mode: operating machinery, driving trucks, and others halfway up telephone poles, digging ditches or tapping on computer keyboards.

The old men I encountered – as they were mostly old men – I felt like getting into conversation, so that I could somehow slip in that I was an artist, an artist who worked from home. I'd let them know that I was sourcing inspiration. That's how I'd put it: 'sourcing inspiration'.

I did not, however, initiate any conversation with them. Only if they greeted me first did I respond with an absent-minded, "Oh. Good morning to you."

As one of these men, being led by his dog, drew near, I adopted what I figured would come across as a dreamy, fascinated air, as I regarded the shifting clouds, the swaying reeds and the bending light playing over the canal's surface.

"That's a grand morning betimes," the old man said. The same thing he usually said about the evening whenever I'd encounter him.

"Oh," I said. "Good morning to you."

"As long as it keeps up, says you." His congenial, round face, crowded with good-fellowship and wobbling with laughter, was irresistible.

We might have been conspirators in a practical joke against all of humanity the way he and I laughed together at nothing.

"Max," he then called over my shoulder. Serious now. "Max, get out of it."

I twisted round to see the old man's dog, a black and white collie, attempting to mount Bruno. And Bruno, like a great oaf, just stood there like he didn't know what he was supposed to do.

"Come here, Bruno," I called to him.

But Bruno jerked his head behind him at the other dog, as though he was afraid to insult him or something by bounding off to me.

A good thirty paces up the bank, the old man and I started back towards the dogs.

"That little bugger," the man said. "Always at the same game. Your fellow's not a bitch, is he?"

"Nope," I said, creasing my eyes and shaking my head, searching for something to say that might diffuse the awkward situation and lessen the jangling feeling in my teeth.

"Get out of it, Max," the old man repeated when we reached the dogs. And he kicked his dog into its ribs. The animal yipped and left off its misguided advances on

Bruno, and then stood there, shuddering, regarding its master with a raised eye and glancing at Bruno with the other. Its black lips trembled.

The old man apologized, while I was snapping the lead onto Bruno's collar.

"Nothing. Don't worry about it, sir." I gave him a wave and started to push off, but now he was ready to really talk. I could tell.

"Lie down, Max," he commanded his collie. "Charlie Cosgrave," he added, extending a wizened, purple hand for me to shake.

"Nice to meet you," I said, taking his hand, except he somehow withdrew it so I was just left gripping his shiny fingers. An instant, unfocused anger bounced about in my head.

"What's this you said your name was?" he asked.

Resisting the confrontational and obvious retort, *I didn't*, I told him my name.

"I knew a fellow by that name once," he said. He pursed his lipless mouth and shifted his watery eyes to something in the canal waters. "Up in Guinness's, you know, back in the days. The fifties. I used to work there meself, you know. Way before your time, mind you."

"Well, Listen," I said, twisting my wrist to look at my watch. "I'd best be pushing on anyway—"

"So, nothing on the work-front?" he said, as though we'd been engaged in that topic.

"I'm an artist. I have my own studio. Work from home. I do commissions," I lied. "Landscapes, animal portraiture. That type of thing."

The old man was shaking his head and making this tisk-tisk sound. "It's hard these days," he said. "My young fellow's the same. Only he's not that young anymore. Thirty-eight. Has a family. Three boys and a girl." His head continued to shake and his compressed mouth put me in mind of an ape behind glass in the zoo.

"No," I said. "Painting. Painting pictures is how I make my living. I'm an artist."

"Plays whatdoyoumecallit all day? Computer games," he went on. "If, that is, he's not – what's this they say? – Loading down them blue movies and the whole lot."

I told him I really had to be pressing on. He didn't move. I left him standing there on the canal bank, lamenting the good old days and shaking his head and repeating that he just didn't get it. He shouted after me that he was sorry for my generation and the whole lot.

When I reached the seventh lock, the place that is usually my turning back point, it occurred to me that I'd be sure to bump into the old guy again should I return the same route as I came. So, instead I cut through the valley that sliced through two housing estates. The journey would be longer, but there was no other way of avoiding old Charlie Cosgrave, as he called himself.

The valley arced along a walled-in tributary connected to the canal. It led, I knew, to a neighbourhood I'd only ever driven through. It took me longer than I'd anticipated.

With the hill up ahead, minutes away, that took me up onto the bridge and into the streets, I decided I'd better get in touch with Margaret and let her know I wasn't going to make it home before she went back to work after lunch. That's when I noticed Bruno wagging his tail good-naturedly at something or someone hidden in the long grass about twenty paces away.

I heard their nasally tones before I saw them: three youths, hunched up at the edge of the worn track. They wore tracksuits with the hoods pulled over their heads. Two of them had white plastic bags in their hands, while the third, also clutching a white bag, was making sucking and blowing sounds into the bag, which was pressed to his face.

"C'mon, Bruno," I said, trying to avoid eye contact with the youths.

Bruno obeyed, bounding on in front of me, until, responding to a sneering voice behind me calling after him, he shot by me and back to the glue-sniffing trio.

"Bruno," I shouted. No use. One of them had grabbed hold of Bruno's collar and was patting his head.

Bruno, I could see, was torn between enjoying the attention of strangers and obeying my command. Either way, he couldn't break loose. Not even when he tried out his favourite trick of crouching down on his front legs in a display to show that he was anxious to take off and be chased.

Not wanting to antagonise the solvent-sniffing trio, I greeted them with a "How's it going, lads?" but I made sure to put a swagger into my step and push out my chest.

"Does he bite, mister?" the one hanging onto Bruno's collar said. His eyes were half-lidded and the eyes themselves seemed to look at me without reference, the way the eyes of a diseased animal might, too sick to flee and too frightened to stir.

"Only when he's angry," I said, snapping the lead in place. "Let's go, Bruno. "C'mon, boy." But one of the other two had now also grabbed onto Bruno's collar.

The fuzzy thought about the effects of solvent abuse on the nervous system wove its way into my instinctive impulse to lash out at these scumbags. The chemicals deadened their senses – that was it. They wouldn't feel a thing.

"Ah hold on there, mister," the second one said. "We only want to ask you a question, like." He pronounced 'ask' as 'axe', which somehow disturbed the hell out of me.

"Hurry up then," I heard myself saying. "I don't have all day to sit around – like some people."

"Now listen here," the first one said, as he got to his feet. "Don't be bleeding smart."

"Yeah," the third one chipped in. "There's no need for that. Alls we want is your odds, is all."

With two of them now on their feet, their outstretched hands, gaunt features and pale pallor transforming them into diseased demons, and the third one struggling to steady himself onto his haunches, my body overrode my reservations.

I struck out and caught the taller of the two a good one between the legs, and with the end of Bruno's lead I lashed the other across the face.

The quick sprint I then made towards the hill and to safety, Bruno cantering next to me on his lead, the air filled with the nasal and guttural snarls coming from the sickly creatures hounding and yet far from closing, all combined together to infuse me with a completely enervating bout of nausea when we made it to our destination.

Ensuring they'd definitely given up the chase, I leaned forward, my legs bent, and rested my hands on my thighs and threw up.

"No, Bruno," I said, dragging him from the mess that had flushed from my insides. Weakly, I pulled him clear. We shoved off for home.

Except, I soon realised I wasn't going to make it home. I felt rotten. My decision to call Margaret and get her to take the rest of the day off – it was, after all, my birthday – and come and collect me was stymied on account of my mobile lying somewhere along the valley between the exit and the point where I assaulted two miserable looking kids who probably weren't more than sixteen.

A drink. I needed to sit down somewhere and have a drink. And poor Bruno too, his long pink tongue flapping in the warm breeze, was likely even more in want of liquid than me.

My lucky day – that's a joke. The first pub along the road for home had a space for chairs and seats outside. A customer leaving the pub very obligingly listened to my story. He'd look after things, he said. He knew the manager. He returned to the pub and came out with the manager.

The manager, a small man with a bald, pinkish plate and an impressive grey moustache, insisted on serving me personally. He complimented Bruno's handsome looks, gave him a long drink in a bucket, and fed him leftovers from the lunch menu.

After a bit, my dizziness left me, but my thirst wouldn't abate.

"Cider is what you need, brother," a chap who'd invited himself to sit with Bruno and me advised. "Cuts right into the thirst." He made a sawing gesture with his hand and whistled the way the wind sometimes whistles.

Turns out this chap was also on Tony's books. He needed the extra few bob to pay the mortgage, he said. By day he worked for the telephone company.

"No way," I said. "Tony? That bastard. You work for him too?"

He made a shushing gesture with his finger to his mouth, and then laughed as though it was the funniest thing in the world. I thought so too, so we ordered some shorts, and laughed some more.

"Are you married yourself?" he asked, although we hadn't been, I didn't think so anyway, talking about women or marriage.

"Whoa. Back up there, man," I said. "I have a wife and a child." I squinted at him to see his face better. He was all blurred.

"What?" he said. "No, no, no, you got me wrong, brother," he said, working himself into a bout of laughter again. "I have a missus too. Malaysia. You want to see her."

He went on to explain that he'd recently got hitched to an Asian bride. Paid her fare over from her own country. She was back home in Malaysia now for some festival or other, some crap, he wasn't sure.

"Just wait until I get her home on Friday," he said. "Whump. She won't know what hit her."

Broken images of the old man's dog with Bruno earlier that day wavered across my unfocused vision. Tumbling through those distasteful images came the faces of the solvent-abusing teenagers.

"I'm going to be sick."

My new friend told me to *hang in there, brother*, and staggered off for the manager.

The manager insisted on driving me home. It was his break-time anyway, he said. As for Bruno, he had a dog of his own. Wasn't a problem. So long as Bruno was housetrained, or car-trained, he quipped.

He got me back home a good hour or so before Margaret pulled into the driveway. In the meantime, I fixed myself a double espresso.

"You've been drinking," she said when she got in. She always says this. I ignored her. She ushered Emer upstairs. She doesn't like Emer seeing me drunk.

"How was work?" I asked, turning from the blank canvas. My head was splitting.

"How could you do this to us?" she said. "A perfectly good job, and you just walk away from it."

I parried that I had work; the security work in the evenings.

"A few hours three or four days a week isn't going to keep this family going," she said.

"I have pictures to paint," I said. "My portfolio wasn't going to get itself together if I stayed on in that kip."

She slumped into the broken armchair and cupped her face in her hands. Here we go.

"You're a lush," she said. "Nothing but a lousy lush." Margaret's American. The first time she called me a lush, it sounded sweet. We laughed long and hard. Neither of us was laughing now.

"The odd glass helps me concentrate," I said. "Gets the muse going."

She was blubbering now. She emerged from her hands.

"Emer is afraid of you," she said. "Your own child."

Something beat at the inside of my head and my scalp felt itchy. "Could be worse. Gauguin left his wife and kids and took off for Tahiti to paint."

What?" she said, and stared at me like I was mad.

"Paul Gauguin. A friend of Van Gogh."

"Didn't he cut off his ear?"

"What? Nobody's cutting their ear off. You're the one who's crazy." She lost it then. Rushed upstairs and screamed herself to sleep in our bedroom.

I called up Tony and told him I wasn't, after all, going in that night. I needed a break. Tony said that was 'game-ball' with him. But he added that I could have as long a break as I wanted, from his company anyway. He closed the call.

When I checked in on Margaret later, she and Emer were asleep together in our bed.

Back downstairs I tried to remember that quote by Van Gogh. Something about how, one day, people would pay more for his paintings than he did for the paint, but that wasn't it exactly. I knew what I meant.

Misunderstood. That's what I was. For a while I contented myself with this self-affirmation. As a misunderstood artist, I was entitled to indulge in what others regarded as eccentricities. I was above their pettiness, their misguided take on behaviour they deemed unacceptable, that didn't conform to their banal understanding of how to be and what to say.

I lay on the couch with these thoughts, flicking from channel to channel, until I hit upon something to get the juices flowing: a little soft porn.

While watching the TV screen, I unconsciously scratched my chin, which reopened the nick I'd given myself that morning while shaving. Working my way round the coffee table to the mirror over the mantelpiece, I tilted my thirty-seven-year-old head sideways. A beautiful, zigzag line of blood, already congealing, ran down my neck.

It came to me then, as my intense reflection stared back at me: Van Gogh was another of the famous thirty-seven-year-olds. Van Gogh, or Vincent, as I liked to call him, was thirty-seven that bright, sunny day when he got himself into one of those glorious, yellow hayfields he had so often painted, placed a rifle barrel against his chest and squeezed the trigger.

Once There Were Rabbits

They're all alike. The faces. The ones that never sleep, the younger ones, dress the same. Winter and summer they keep on their long white coats. They look like a gang of turkeys, their feathers whiter than white. They forget who they are; so pinned to their coats are badges with their names.

The other faces, the ones that hatch overnight in the beds, are old and wrinkled. The older faces are kept as pets by younger ones. The younger faces feed them. Put on and take off their clothes. Sometimes they bring them for walks. But the older faces can't stay away too long from their beds. Keep them away for too long and they wail and scream. The terrible sounds they make, some crying out for their mammies, is like the screeching of tomato plants removed too soon from a glasshouse.

Then there are faces that don't belong in this house. My house. There's that woman whose hair is as red as a fox. If you close your eyes and open them, there she is.

She's here again, now. The woman. She's after my notebook. I pretend to be asleep. Maybe I am asleep. She doesn't try to wake me. I can smell her. She smells like daisies in summertime. Or the grass after rain – is it? I feel her lips pressed to my cheek. She tells me not to cry. Must have been crying in my sleep. Probably I was dreaming about Annie. The way she used to be. I don't remember.

Annie went away sometime. Christmas Eve, I think it was, or the summer maybe. I don't know. The pictures are in black and white. He took her. But she hasn't really left. Annie. I mean, she's returned. I see her driving around inside this house in that little car she has. She's changed her face, and her height too. Annie used to be tiny. Now she's taller than me even. Trying to fool them she is. She spies on me when the fox-haired woman is here. Makes herself invisible, but I can feel her in the room. I keep my eyes closed. That way she can't be sure I'm there.

Before Annie left, there was just the three of us – Annie, me, and a girl. As pale as paper the girl's skin, except for freckles. And she had ginger hair. There was a baby as well, but it got lost. The girl played in the garden. There were rabbits. Annie took the garden with her. So the rabbits are gone, and the girl disappeared, too. That's when this house grew bigger. You'd go to sleep, and when you woke up there'd be new rooms.

Because of Annie, this house is full of faces. She brought them back with her. Most of the faces are old and sad. Some of them try to speak with me. I keep my eyes closed and they go away.

When I have to leave my bed, I wear dark glasses. My eyes are hidden. Nobody sees me. I can look right at Annie – the new Annie. She's beautiful. I say to her, "The lights are still on, Annie. I've kept the lights on. Like you said." She doesn't answer.

We're going to get married again. But the faces can't know. That's why Annie doesn't talk to me. It's a secret. The faces are jealous. Annie too. She always was. So I speak to nobody else. Except when I have to.

The younger faces here aren't so easily fooled. They want to control the other faces. They can see in the dark with their special vision. Even when I squeeze my eyes closed, they know I'm there. Invisibility doesn't work against the younger faces. They just prod you and tell you to wake up. If you don't eat, they pinch your nose and your mouth opens. The food they push down your throat is cold and mushy.

I don't care for food anymore. It tastes funny. That's the poison. But I'm wise to their caper. I drink water right through the night. I love the night-time and darkness. I take the water from the sleeping faces. At night-time, I put on my invisible cloak and move around the room, gulping down the glasses of iceberg water. Sometimes a face wakes up, obviously terrified at the sight of a floating glass. I snap my invisible hand over its mouth. "Make any noise," I say, "and I'll kill the TV forever." That shuts them up. The faces love the TV. It's their energy source; what keeps them alive.

My head hurts today. I need to look in the mirror to find the pain. But that woman's sitting by my bed. To open my eyes would be to fall under her spell. I can hear her prattling on about the new Annie not being Annie. Besides her, there are too many younger faces about. They're restless. Just waiting for me to slip away from the herd. It's the straggler that always gets it. I won't move until it's dark.

Their smell makes them vulnerable. It's their weakness. One night I'll track them down, find out how they get their power, and take their seeing eyes from them. Without their eyes, they'll turn into the other faces. Then, when all the faces are connected to the TV in the room that smells like hippopotamuses, I'll kill the TV and watch them melt.

It'll be just me and Annie again, the way it was before the faces. Before the baby and the blinding lights. And the girl will be there, and the garden, and what else? I don't remember sometimes. The poison takes away the pictures. Not all the poison is washed away by the water.

There was water in the garden. A pool. And trees. When I squeeze my eyes shut, I can transport myself back to the garden.

The girl is there. And Annie. The old Annie. She's putting down bulbs for springtime before the frost. She can't see me because I'm coming from the other place and I have my cloak. She knows the names of all the flowers. I never remember. My favourite ones are the red ones that look like they've been dipped in fried eggs.

Annie is distracted today – more than usual. The girl is playing at the end of the garden. That's where the brambles and nettles grow. They've taken over. One time there was a path. That was before the girl. At the end of the path was a gate into the laneway. Annie was afraid of that gate when the girl came to the garden. Annie was happy when the garden swallowed up the path.

The girl is having tea in the grass with her invisible friend. The girl and me are the only ones who can see her invisible friend. He's the missing baby who got lost in the garden. I remember how the girl was playing in the garden with the baby. Annie was in work. She was a teacher. A fire burned in the sky that day. Sweat trickled down my forehead and made my eyes itchy. I kept rubbing them, trying to see the girl properly, while she was laughing and telling me about the baby crawling under the scratchy things. I ran to the end of the garden. The girl ran with me. But the baby had vanished. The girl said she'd heard a man's voice behind the gate. Annie believed her. Me and the girl know what really happened.

The fairies. The fairies took the baby. He lives with them still in a rabbit burrow beneath the blackberry bushes. Annie often woke up at night-time, shivering, babbling about how she heard his baby-talk and laugh. I'd tell her it was her imagination, and I used to hold her and sing to her so she couldn't hear the baby dancing and singing on the lawn with his fairy family.

In the daytime, the baby comes to play with the girl. I study them on my visits and make notes in my notebook. I listen to them talking. They don't know I'm there. I heard him tell her how he mustn't be seen by anyone, or the king of the fairies will punish him, so the baby becomes invisible. I learned how to make myself invisible by listening to the girl and the baby talking.

The fairy king needs a new wife. His queen has flown away. That's what the baby told the girl. At first I thought he was going to take the girl, too, but it's Annie he's after. My queen. Only he can't just snatch her the way he did the baby. She has to choose to go with him because she wants to. That's the reason he took the baby – to keep Annie in the garden. Annie is obsessed with her garden.

She doesn't teach anymore. Annie. Spends every day pulling weeds, planting seeds and turning the earth. Every so often she stops, cocks her head sideways like a bird and seems to listen. She calls out the baby's name, waits for an answer, and then her mouth moves without words at the earth.

The girl has tried to coax Annie into the house in bad weather. May as well try to unplug the winter. The baby got lost in the daytime, so it'll be daytime when he returns. She'll be waiting for him. That's Annie's logic.

If it weren't for the girl, there'd be no dinner in the evening for either of them. I have my job and am away all the time. That's it, isn't it? I'm confused. Anyway, she looks after Annie now. Does everything. Brings her in when it's getting dark. Annie says it's hard to tell the difference. The lights in the garden and from the house make it feel like daytime. She listens to the girl. Annie's afraid of the dark. Never slept until after we got the lights put in outside. I remember.

"What if the baby makes his way home?" she says. This isn't a question for me, the 'me' I used to be, or for the girl. "It has to be daytime when he comes," she says. "The lights must never go off. The lights must never go off." She repeats this like a mantra. If Annie falls into one of her trances, the ginger-haired girl tries to shush her. She embraces her and kisses her cheek. “He’s with Holy God, Mom, okay?” the girl whispers up to Annie,” “He won’t be coming home ever.”

Strange. The woman who comes to me in the big house and tries to steal my notebook says the same thing about Annie. I must have mentioned Annie in my sleep just now because I feel the woman’s breath on my face. She’s whispering those words again.

“She’s in heaven, Dad. Mom has left the lights on. They’re waiting for you.”

Ruler of the Roost

Like a murderer expecting his next victim, he waits. Wedded to the moment before his blade sears flesh and blood splashes hotly, soaking his killing hands with satiated lust and love.

On his hunkers, twelve-year-old Lewis holds Barney in his lap. He grips lightly the cockerel's scaly legs, and strokes the bird's inflated breast, while speaking to him soft words that calm the flighty creature. Accustomed to each other, boy and bird have been sitting together in this position for a number of minutes, when Chase, his father's black and white collie, gambols down the slope that leads to the chicken coop entrance. Behind the dog Lewis's younger cousin, Dudley, known to all except Dudley's mother as Dud.

Barney struggles in the boy's arms, and gives his drawn-out warning cry, which sends the hens into a squawking and flapping sprint for cover. The boy makes shushing sounds and tightens his hold on the bird.

"Lie down, Chase," Lewis's father's voice calls from the top of the slope. "Come here, lad."

"Get 'em," Dudley whispers. "Kill it, Chase."

The collie spins round on its hind legs, and crouches to the ground, before dashing back up the trail, its pink ribbon of tongue whipping over its white-blazoned muzzle. Lewis's father snarls at the dog. It crouches to heel.

"Stay," his father commands the dog as he opens and enters the coop. "You too, Dud. Close that door behind me there."

His father glances at Lewis without speaking. He then takes a few long strides across the coop to the laying boxes. Stooping down he picks up a bedraggled, half-plucked and bleeding Rhode Island Red hen wedged beneath one of the boxes. Holding the bird aloft by the legs, he steps closer to Lewis. Barney sounds his disapproval. Lewis feels the cockerel's strength as the bird fights for freedom against his protective embrace.

"Okay, mind me now, boy," his father says. And, in a lesson he has given Lewis before, he runs his free hand down the chicken's neck to the base of its head, grips tightly and pulls hard.

Outside the mesh wire of the enclosure, Dudley is jumping up and down, laughing a high-pitched laugh.

While the dead bird thrashes about, Lewis's father holds it close to his own body. His eyes the whole time he keeps on Lewis. Lewis, in turn, is unable to pull his gaze from the creature's death throes until it stops moving. Only then does he realise he has increased his hold on Barney enough to cause the struggling bird obvious discomfort. He loosens his grip on its legs. That's when he feels a slashing sting in his torso just below his chest, where one of the cockerel's spurs catches him through his T-shirt. He releases the bird.

Barney runs a few paces, flaps and clambers up the side of a laying box. There he stretches his proud neck skywards and crows three times – one crow for each of his slain flock.

"Go get him," Lewis's father says. "He's your bird."

"Get him, Lewis," Dudley echoes. "Go get him. Stretch his stupid neck." And he clenches his teeth and mimes his uncle killing the hen.

A wave of nausea sloshes about Lewis's stomach. Behind his eyes a staccato rhythm beats in time to the thrumming in his ears.

"I don't feel too good," he says. He works himself to his feet, one hand pressed against his stomach, the other massaging his temples. He starts for the door.

"Don't you walk away from me, boy."

Lewis freezes.

"And speak like a man, not like some half-baked, stuttering and stammering idiot," he adds.

Peripherally Lewis watches his father sidle up to Barney. Quick as a professional boxer, he strikes out and grasps the cockerel by the legs. The bird squawks in vain. But, defeated, he hangs upside down in the man's hand, his round wings drooping at the earth.

"Take him," he says to Lewis. "To be a man, you have to act like a man."

Lewis shakes his head. "M-m-maybe he won't attack any m-more of them."

"He's turned," his father says. "Once they get a taste for it, there's no changing them. I've seen it before."

Lewis feels his own arms rising to receive his pet cockerel.

"No. By the legs. Take his legs." He adjusts his own grip so Lewis can grasp Barney's thick legs. "Right. Now put your hand around his neck."

Lewis does as he is instructed. Barney's neck is soft and warm. His familiar chicken smell pervades his senses.

"Now slide your hand down to the back of his head. Okay. That's it. Then turn your hand. No. The other way, with your palm facing you. Okay, you have it. And this is the important part. You don't want to cause him any suffering. You're going to pull down hard till you feel a sort of pop. That's when the job is done."

Lewis sees himself carrying out his father's instructions as he gives them. He can anticipate how the popping in his hand would feel when Barney's head separates from his spine. He sees the bird's blinking, disbelieving eyes, his open beak and protruding tongue. But the weight of the bird on his extended arm is too great. He places the cockerel gently on his side in the dusty earth. Barney flaps to his feet, ruffles his feathers, and struts away.

"What're you doing, boy? This is not a game," his father shouts at him.

Inside his stomach Lewis feels a tightening hand squeezing the way his fingers have held Barney's legs. The hand increases its grip. Unable to resist the pressure, Lewis tastes hot bitter bile surging into his mouth. And from his lips spills his half-digested breakfast.

Responding to Barney's clucking summoning, the cockerel's harem come rushing and squawking to feast on the unexpected meal.

As Lewis groans and walks feebly towards the coop door, this time his father says nothing. Instead, he spits into the floor, screws up his face and shakes his head. Dudley makes chicken noises after Lewis.

"Shut up, Dud," Lewis's father says. "Get back to your own house."

From his bedroom that evening, Lewis hears his mother and father going at each other in their usual manner. He slips out of his bed and creeps down the first few steps so he can hear them better.

"I never touched him," he hears his father repeat.

"You did something," his mother says. "His stutter's worse than ever."

There follows silence. Lewis imagines his father standing before the mirror, shifting his head about at different angles, admiring the scar that runs from his left eye almost to his jaw. A mark left by a horse's hoof.

"Somebody needs to toughen him up."

"What? I thought you said you didn't go near him?"

"I didn't."

"No? Like those times you didn't force him to take hold of the electric fence?"

"The jolts are good for him. Knock that jabbering out of him."

"A bully. All his life you've bullied that boy. Pushed him around and bullied him for not being like you."

Lewis hears a dull thumping sound, his father's fist hammering down on the table or sideboard.

"Jesus Christ."

"Don't you start your banging and smashing things around here. I'm calling your brother if you keep at this now."

"Look. Everything here will be his one day. I've kept this place going through sweat and hard work so as I can pass it on to him, the way my old man did for me."

"I've listened to this a million times. I'm sick of it."

Lewis has heard it too, and knows what's coming next. He clenches his teeth till his jaw throbs.

"Good for you," his father says to his mother. "Good for you. But let me ask you this – How the hell can I pass it on to that fella when he hasn't even got the spunk to climb onto a horse's back?"

Lewis fights against the compelling urge to stay where he is, to remain and hear again his father's terrible words. His willpower loses. He stays.

"Why can't you just let him be?" he hears his mother say.

"I swear to God," his father says. "Sometimes I wonder if he's actually my own son."

"Bastard."

Lewis feels in his throat an instant hollowness. He swallows. In his head, blurred snapshots flashing broken images of himself as a small boy following his father into the milking parlour. His father's big and comforting laugh protecting him from the lowing and grunting cows. That protective laugh surrounding him too when he stood in front of his daddy in the tractor cabin, as they drove round the field next to the stream. The secrets they shared. The wishes they made when they dropped the coins into the dark well beneath the aspen grove, the trees' leaves trembling without breeze. Lewis's constant wish back then was that he would one day take to the air like a bird and fly. His single wish now is that he could return to his early childhood and remain forever a little boy.

Back in bed and unable to reach the temporary refuge of sleep, Lewis does what he always does – he concentrates hard and imagines himself into someone else's world. Usually he fantasises himself into one of his sporting or superheroes, Lionel Messi and the Hulk being his favourites. Sometimes he becomes Bear Grylls, dropping from a helicopter, an island pinpricked in a kingfisher-blue ocean below. This time he becomes Barney, the proud and strutting ruler of the chicken coop, the pet cockerel his father almost forced him to slaughter.

He imagines himself as the white cockerel turned hen-killer.

Highly-strung, watcher over his feathered flock, their safety depends on Barney's diligence. Keeper of Harmony, the watcher becomes the watched. Early morning.

Barney is the first to leave the shelter of the night-time roost. A few tentative steps and clucks, he tilts his crowned head one way then the other, checking the brightening sky for marauding hawks. None. All about him the aggressive twittering of inferior birds, sounding claim to territory. A few emboldened flaps and he scrabbles atop the henhouse. Another check skyward, he then stretches his neck, opens his beak and crows his dominance at his unseen partner, the wind. The wind in coalition carries Barney's voice across the fields, through the trees and downstream. Silence now. All twittering and singing ceases, the leaves in the trees quit fluttering. Even the stream leaves off its babbling. All wait, as does Barney. Then in the distance a challenger answers his crowing.

Through his muscular being Barney feels his challenger's disrespect. Barney's harem emerges into the day, the young Rhode Island Red leading the flock. In response to the neighbouring cockerel, Barney crows again. As he expects, the challenger responds. Every feather on Barney's body stands on edge. Were his enemy on front of him, he'd tear him asunder. But wait? He spies something among his own flock, the first sign of betrayal that undermines who he is and what he is for. The Rhode Island Red is on top of the red barrel drum craning her neck in the direction of the distant and unseen cockerel.

In a rage, Barney opens his stubby wings and jumps from atop the henhouse. His vision now soaked in blood, he makes for the offending hen. Except, she is no longer one of his flock. Her disloyalty has transformed her into the unreachable enemy. He falls upon her, his neck feathers splayed like a crown. He pecks and tears at her back. He lifts himself from the ground and slashes downwards with his spurs. And he keeps worrying the terrified bird until her squawking gives out and she accepts defeat and waits for the tall creature known to all the birds and beasts as 'Death'. The creature who feeds them and ultimately decides who lives and when they die.

The next morning Lewis awaits Dudley's usual arrival after breakfast. Dudley and his family are holidaying in Lewis's parents' guesthouse next door. Lewis sits outside on the wooden decking. Dudley arrives with a homemade catapult.

"What's that for?" Lewis asks.

Dudley pulls back the elastic and points in Lewis's face. "What's that for?" Dudley mimics. He lets the elastic go.

Lewis screams.

"There's nothing it, ye moron, ye," Dudley says, laughing in an even higher pitch than normal.

Dudley tells Lewis that he's made the catapult to take practice shots at Barney. "I'm going to knock his big stupid head off. My ma said she couldn't sleep last night with that thing. Anytime someone turned on the light in the bathroom, that dopey bird thought it was morning."

"He's my bird. If anybody's going to kill him, it's me." Lewis starts off down the trail that leads to the chicken coop.

Dudley trips after him, squawking like a chicken, and daring him, and saying that he bets he wouldn't. He says that everyone knows that Lewis is just a big chicken himself. Dudley's father says so. He laughs, flaps about using his arms like wings, and does a poor impression of a crowing cock.

"My dad says you're just a gibbering gobshite."

Lewis ignores his taunts.

Outside the chicken coop, Lewis picks up a few pebbles.

"What're you doing?" Dudley asks.

Lewis tells him he's collecting ammo for the catapult. Better to stun Barney first with a good shot to the head.

"Deadly," Dudley says, jumping up and down.

"Give me that," Lewis says.

Laughing like someone practicing how to be a maniac, Dudley hands over his homemade catapult. Lewis snaps it from him and, without removing his eyes from his cousin's, tosses the weapon back over his head into the chicken pen. Barney makes the drawn-out, grating sound he uses to warn of imminent danger from four-footed predators.

Lewis smiles.

Dudley frowns.

Tucking his fists under his own armpits, Lewis makes a few tentative clucking sounds and flaps his bent arms. He then drops one arm the way Barney lowers his wing when displaying dominance over unruly hens or younger male chickens. He follows this with a kind of bird waltz, making little tapping steps in a circle around Dudley.

"Get away from me, ye gibbering gobshite, ye."

Lewis moves in rapid steps towards Dudley. Dudley backs from him and tries to push him away. Lewis smacks the other's arm with his, clucks louder and drives him backwards till Dudley's up against the raised bank surrounding the field in which the herd of jersey cows graze. Sensing that Dudley is about to flee, he grasps him by the wrist.

Dudley lets out a scream too high-pitched for a boy it seems to Lewis. "Let me go. Let me go. Dad, help, Dad…"

The backhanded blow that catches Dudley across the jaw and knocks him into the dirt track sends electric impulses shooting up Lewis's arm. "You keep your mouth shut," he says, standing over Dudley, his balled fist raised behind his head. He tells Dudley to stay as he is in the road on his back. With his eyes snared on the cowering Dudley, Lewis steps up the bank and takes in his hand one of the electric fence wire-strands. The dull shock that pumps into his hand and up his arm and jolts his shoulder is deeply satisfying. Maintaining the grin he's practised before the bathroom mirror, he climbs down from the bank.

"Now you. Get up and grab it."

Dudley shakes his head and begs Lewis to let him go. He wipes his hand across his face, leaving a blackened smear.

Lewis kicks him in the side. "Up, I said. Now." He kicks him again harder. In his head flash images of the insolent Rhode Island Red recoiling under Barney's punishment. He bends down and clutches Dudley by the scruff with both hands and jerks him to his feet. "Go on, take it in your hand." In his ear he hears and echoes his father's words. "You don't want to stay a wimp all your life, do you?" Keeping Dudley on his feet with his left hand, he punches him in the shoulder with his right hand. Something his father has done with him. He continues to punch him, increasing the force on every blow. And he punctuates the blows with words: "To-be-a-man-you have-to-learn-to-act-like-a-man."

Taking Dudley by the wrist, the way his father once took his, Lewis steps up the bank, and grips and enfolds again his fingers around the live wire. Dudley lets out a piercing scream as the electric jolt travels from Lewis's body into his.

From the chicken coop behind them Barney crows his defiant crow.

No Understand Nothing

The faces. The usual stupid faces crowd the carriage with threat. Many of them are laughing and talking big now that work or school is finished for the week. I ignore them, including the ones whose language I can understand, the ones from my own country. I stay good alone. I prefer to be with someone when I choose to be with them.

I'm looking out the window at the coastline, allowing the sight of the lapping tide to smooth away the wrinkles of the day, when this fat person, a guy in his early twenties, sitting opposite me says something. About to respond the way I do to everybody in this country, 'No understand nothing', I stop myself.

The fat guy isn't speaking to me. Although he's looking directly into my eyes, his arms gesticulating and his fingers snapping, he's singing along breath for breath to the rap song playing too loud on his Smartphone.

The fool, as white as goat's milk, apart for his red-apple cheeks, thinks he's a black rapper. And I'm his audience.

A heated itchiness attacks my scalp. And when he stretches out his leg, resting his foot on the seat next to my black satchel bag, the urge to strike out at him, to connect my fists with his neck and head until my grazed knuckles sting and bleed is irresistible. Nonetheless, I resist – too public.

I've heard enough stories in this country during the months I've worked construction. Besides, I couldn't even explain myself through lies if I ended up before a judge. Almost two and a half years since I made the long crossing on two ferries, and my ability with this accursed language hasn't progressed beyond simple greetings, and basic requests in shops, stuff I parrot right out of my language manual and CD.

Even so, when his foot shifts, bringing it to rest against my bag, I jerk my head sideways, frown at his heavy-looking trainer with the laces tied beneath the trainer's tongue, and then stare back into his mug. I make one of those faces I've practised before the bathroom mirror.

That gets him. He lifts his leg carefully off the seat, picks up a tatty copy of *The Metro*, tones down his rapping, and leafs through its pages for the next ten minutes before my stop.

Getting out from my seat, I deliberately and forcefully brush against his leg. He mutters something that might be an apology or an insult. The tone suggests an apology. I affect a fleeting grin and crease my eyes. "You're a very lucky man," I say to him in my own language.

He nods, his mouth pursed in a whistling shape.

Clutching my satchel bag to my side, and waiting at the door, the train seems to brake suddenly and lurch a bit at a level crossing, before moving on. There is the sound of voices at the far end of the carriage. I twist round to see a woman picking herself up off the floor. She answers one or two concerned voices, and makes her way towards my end of the carriage.

She looks embarrassed and seems in a hurry to escape the do-gooders.

I study her as she comes towards me. She keeps her eyes locked to the floor. Her blonde hair is streaked with obvious black roots, and in her lip, nose and eyebrow are silver piercings. I feel something beating at my temples, and I towel my sweaty palms on my black canvas bag.

I want her.

The train stops and the doors whoosh open. I let her step out before me so I can check her out from behind. The short high-pitched cry she makes and the way she presses her hand against her lower back on the platform are the actions that draw us together, that precipitate our union.

With her eyes squeezed shut in her screwed-up face, the woman speaks softly to herself.

"Poland?" I say to her in English.

Her eyes spring open.

"You are Poland?" I ask.

"Yes," she says. And she says something else I don't understand.

"I am Latvia," I say.

More from her body language than what she says, I gather she wants to be left alone for a bit. She's in pain from the fall.

I sit down on the bench beside her. It seems the right thing to do. Staring straight ahead, I rest my hands on my thighs until the woman's pain lessens. Pain always goes away eventually. And it does.

Turns out she, like me, has been taught Russian in school. My Russian is slightly better than hers, which gives me the confidence I need to ask her all the questions you're supposed to ask women.

She's been in Ireland for less than a month. She misses her family and friends. For now, she works as a nanny in a three-storey house with a garden that is a mini park. She smiles saying this, but her smile is terribly sad. The parents of the three boys she looks after expect her to do everything. That's why she stays out the whole day on her days off. Otherwise the boys' parents, especially the mama, would get her to mind the boys while she works on the computer from home. Or watch them in the supermarket while she shops, or even clean up their room while the boys ransack it.

Why do these types of people have children, she wants to know. She doesn't expect an answer, so I shrug.

I'm trying to figure out how to get this girl to come with me, not to my part of the city, where people know me to see, but I have the exact spot in mind, a place I haven't been to for a while, when she comes right out and suggests we go get something to eat. There's a Polish restaurant, she gushes, where a friend of hers works. He gives her extra food.

The way her face alters from unhappiness to a bright glow talking about this *friend* claws at the inside of my head.

I never eat this early, I tell her. I suggest we go for a drink first – I need one. I know a quiet Irish pub along the canal not far from the station, I tell her. She hesitates. I affect an indifferent gesture by turning down my mouth. It works. I've seen guys do this in movies.

The pub is almost empty. Mostly a few old men whose watery eyes flick at you once, and once only. The barman, a young-old man with greying red hair, keeps his eyes on me longer than he should.

We sit at the bar on stools. She says she prefers a table.

"Sure," I say. Whatever it takes.

I order and then follow her to a small table with soft chairs. I glance back at the barman after a minute. He nods for me to collect the drinks, a pint of lager for me, and a Miller Lite for her. The barman doesn't say "Thanks" when I pay him.

"You're welcome," I say in Latvian.

Placing her drink before her, I tell her she can spot me for that another day.

"What?" she says.

"Nothing," I say. "It's a joke."

She excuses herself to visit 'the ladies'.

I bounce back up to the bar and order a shot of something stronger. I make sure to throw an eye back on my satchel sitting on the seat. The barman serves me reluctantly, it seems. He leans across the counter and says something to me wearing this face, his hands pressed palm-down on the countertop. His nose is wrinkled and his mouth twisted, as if he is trying to block out the stench of putrid flesh. He knows me. I've been here only a few times before, but he remembers me.

"Cheers," I say in English, and knock back my drink.

The woman returns and we sit back down. She wants to know about me, how old I am. Thirty-one, I lie. My family? All dead except one brother back home, and I've fallen out with him a long time ago. The truth.

"Do you know many Polish people here?" I ask her, just to break away from the interrogation.

She's travelled over with a bunch of friends. They hook-up at weekends, but she's fed up with the partying and the drinking. She's more interested in meeting people, exploring the city and learning about the culture and music.

"And your boyfriend?" I ask. A nerve taps at the side of my head.

"What about him?"

I'm right.

"Does he, you know, work evenings and stuff when you're off? How do you… When do you—"

"My boyfriend is in Poland. He calls me all the time on my mobile." She slips a pink phone from her bag. "I keep it turned off."

Why have I assumed the guy in the restaurant was her boyfriend?

"And you. You look like a man who is married."

Instant anger infuses me at the idea that I have a married-look about me, as though girls wouldn't find me attractive.

I laugh and shake my head. Her eyes do a semi-circle around the bar and then drop to her glass. She picks it up and sucks in a few small sips, hardly tipping the glass backwards. She reminds me of a pigeon drinking from a puddle.

By the time we leave the pub it's dark. She refuses my invitation for a walk along the canal banks. She's up early in the morning for the children. She has to get home. Besides, her host parents would be wondering where she is. She was supposed to be home by seven.

"They'll think I am out eating men," she says, with a forced laugh. "The father, he already thinks I'm a bitch."

The smouldering fire in the pit of my stomach sends flames shooting to my head. And my fingertips tingle. "Why?" I say, playing for time. "Why does he think that?"

She knows, she explains, by the way his eyes slide around her body at the breakfast table, as soon as the mama goes upstairs to get ready. And, a few times in the car, when he drove her and the boys to the park, he took his hand from the gear-stick and rested it on her thigh, supposedly to make some point. Here she places her own hand on herself, and her skirt rides up her leg a few inches.

"Listen," I say. We're beneath one of those period lampposts and I can't be sure there's no one about.

"What?" She shakes her head and smiles. "What are we listening for?"

I shush her with my finger to my mouth. "Come." I take her hand in mine. She lets me take it. My satchel swings between us as I lead her down the unlit path to the bench by the water's edge. "Let me get this out of the way." I remove my bag and plop it onto the bench.

"You're silly." Too dark to make out her features clearly now, I hear a smile in her voice.

The punch I slam into the side of her face takes her by surprise. The first punch gets them every time. The second blow into the stomach winds her, preventing her from screaming out. Quickly I locate by touch what I need from my already opened bag and go to work on the female struggling to scramble off the ground.

I gag her first with the industrial tape, encircling her head twice to be sure. I then bind her hands behind her back. Her legs I leave untied. A mistake I made one time only, the first time.

I listen again. Except for the odd car on the other side of the bank, silence. I then inhale deeply the scent rising from her body, the greatest of all aphrodisiacs, the pungent smell of fear.

Melanie's Little Garden

She no longer questioned him. Easier to fake sleep than to suffer his lies. That way Janice gave herself no excuse to leave the warmth of their double bed for the icy sheets draped over the narrow bed in Melanie's room. She could hear the faint yapping of the puppies rising through the ceiling from downstairs. His arriving in late had disturbed them again. From its cardboard box in the corner of the bedroom, Sheba, the rejected puppy, yipped and yapped in response; a racket that would continue until he finished up in the bathroom and came to bed.

Through half-open eyelids, Janice watched his silhouette slip out of the bath towel and into his pyjamas. He mumbled something nasty to himself about the 'stupid dog' in the corner stinking up the place.

The late-night showers were what first made her suspicious – though her initial suspicions were diluted by vague curiosity. Her mind seldom wandered far from its main preoccupation: Melanie.

It had started over a month back. How casually she had put it to him then. How come he didn't shower at the club?

He hadn't had the time, he snapped.

No time? It was after two in the morning.

So he'd played on till closing time. Mixed doubles. So what? By then the changing rooms were locked up.

And how did that explain the hour he was getting in?

"Jesus. What do you want from me?" he asked. "Can I not go for a few drinks with the guys from the club anymore?"

Out of their bed she bounded, slammed the door behind her, and into Melanie's unheated room. As soon as she got the blood flowing back into her feet and hands, she spoke to Melanie.

"Hi Sweetie. Mommy's back." And she picked up, from memory, where she left off that evening reading one of Melanie's favourite stories. But what she had earlier, in daylight, used as a way to shuck off the horrors of reality, now, in the solitary depths of night-time, crowded her senses, though inversely, with everything that had constituted Melanie, her seven-year-old child's short existence.

Absent was Melanie's giggling and piping voice reciting, breath for breath with Janice, favourite lines spoken by the story's fairy-tale princess. No more that bright-eyed face staring at the imaginary images conjured up by the story. And gone, too, the honeyed milkiness released from her daughter's skin when she pressed her lips to the little girl's soft, sleeping face.

Apart from the shock that he might be betraying her with another woman, Janice couldn't accept Geoff's callousness. Only a few weeks back he'd forgotten Melanie's birthday, and had accused Janice of being 'creepy' when she produced the birthday cake with the eight candles and insisted they sing *Happy Birthday*. The Saturday morning trips to the cemetery, too, Janice now made without him. For company she took with her Sheba, the rejected puppy, which she wheeled in Melanie's old pram.

Lately Geoff had become worse.

For Geoff, Melanie may as well never have existed. That's how Janice saw it. Any allusion to their daughter or mention of her name he met with a blank, bovine stare. While Janice continued to move through each day as though Melanie were still in it, Geoff entered a world where pleasure seemed the reigning principle. At weekends he slept on till after midday. Ignoring Janice, when she spoke of how 'Melanie's little garden' was doing, he took out his mobile, stabbed at it, waited a bit, and then ordered in pizza. The pizza he devoured with a half-dozen cans of beer, sitting in his underwear before the afternoon's sports features on TV. The rest of the day he kind of played with the puppies and the bitch. Or he simply padded aimlessly about the house in his bare feet, breaking incongruously into operatic gibberish from time to time.

Not since Melanie was an infant had Janice known Geoff to really take so much pleasure in singing. Not even when they'd first discovered that everything they had done and experienced before fate had brought them together was akin to a prolonged gestation period, could she recall Geoff singing with such fire in his belly.

Crazy even to imagine it, but it was as if the day Melanie ended brought with it the release Geoff hadn't known he'd been awaiting. But how could this be? If anything, Melanie's arrival in the world eight years ago confirmed what Janice already knew: Geoff and she were brought together for a reason. Destiny had seen to it. A reason that went far beyond a perpetual hunger for each other – an appetite whose emptiness grew greater still, the more their lives intertwined. The reason was Melanie. She, Melanie, had chosen them as her parents.

No father had ever cared more for his daughter. That Melanie came into the world with a crippling illness, with bones so brittle, the child would be denied the regular life granted to other children, served only to magnify Geoff's love for their baby girl.

He sat up with the little girl those nights when her tiny frame no longer responded to strong medication. With his back supported by the cushioned headrest on her bed, he enveloped Melanie's agonised body in his dark-skinned, capable hands, his natural tenor voice – the voice of God – singing away their little girl's unjust pain.

Like Janice, Geoff's fatalistic belief in the power of goodness rejected the doctors' prognosis. At birth, the medical people gave the child three or four years at best. No, Geoff agreed with Janice, those times they so often clung onto each other's bodies at night, until it was impossible to determine where her body ended and Geoff's began. Melanie was born to live.

Had not mountains been moved? Unsightly scars healed? The blind granted the gift of sight? So many miracles unexplained, that left science baffled. When pitched against the might of God, science and medicine were nothing.

Now, of course, Janice knew there was no God. What manner of god condemns an unborn child to seven years of agonised nights when only her profound faith in God's love prevented Janice from taking Melanie in her arms and holding her so close, and for so long, she might squeeze away the hurt and deliver to Him the sweetest of angels.

"There's a man coming tomorrow about the last of the pups," Geoff said as soon as he'd settled himself beneath the duvet.

"What?" she said, breaking her self-imposed rule not to answer him when he came in late, stinking of sour wine. An instant wave of nausea churned about inside her. She felt her heart quail.

"He wants them..." – he yawned disinterestedly – "for watchdogs, you know? Your man who has the pub near the church."

Janice sat up. "And Sheba?"

"You can't keep it," he said. His tone was now serious and alert.

"She needs me. I'm taking care of her."

The puppy had managed to somehow hurl itself from

the box and was dragging itself across the darkened room. Its crying for attention was the wailing of a baby.

"Jesus Christ. How the hell am I supposed to get any sleep with that thing?"

"Leave her alone," Janice screamed.

But his silhouette was already out of bed, had scooped Sheba up and vanished into the blast of light that burst in from the landing, by the time Janice had rolled over and got out on his side of the bed. From inside Melanie's closed door, Geoff shouted out and cursed.

"I stubbed my fucking toe," he said, as he stepped out of the room and turned the key in the door. He pushed past Janice.

"What are you doing?" Janice screamed. "You can't lock her in. She's afraid of the dark."

Her hysterical, screaming voice, and the terrifying sense of desperation that gripped her, affected Janice as though she were outside whom she was, watching herself through someone else's eyes. Likewise, the first blow of her head smashing against the door to Melanie's bedroom she experienced as a blinding white light, but felt no pain. The second blow she aimed at the wooden door was cushioned by Geoff's hand.

From behind, Geoff twisted her round and locked her in his arms. She was trapped. Her struggling, her screams, and clawing at his face with her fingernails were in vain.

She spat into his eyes, sunk her teeth into his shoulder until she tasted his warm, salty blood oozing into her mouth, and all the time his voice remained calm. He shushed her as though she were a disturbed child.

Finally, she was exhausted. Geoff half-carried her and led her back into their room and double bed. With the little energy left to her, Janice pleaded with him to at least turn back on the landing light and open Melanie's door slightly. Sheba might wake up and find herself alone in the dark.

“He’s offered to put her to sleep,” he said.

“No, please. You can’t.” She pressed her hand to his cheek. His beard sent excited prickles through her palm as he slid his mouth into the cup of her palm and kissed it gently. In whispered tones he explained that the publican grew up on a farm. He knew about these things. There’d be no suffering. Keeping her alive was unfair on the little mite. She was in constant pain.

“She’s better off dead. You have to accept it, Janice. Be brave.”

Janice. He’d used her name. She’d forgotten how her name sounded in his mouth. Had he, too, forgotten how her name tasted on his tongue?

“Say my name again, Geoff.”

He shushed her and she felt his warm fingers brush aside the strands of hair clinging to her forehead. “Please,” she said.

He eased himself atop her, straddling her, supporting his weight with his knees and outstretched arms. His warm, manly smell, heavy and dark, pervaded her senses.

From the spare room the puppy began to whine.

“Janice,” he whispered next to her ear, his breath tickling and exciting. She, like her body, surrendered.

A collage of broken images and hazy memories flitted and darted around in her head as Geoff’s gentle hands wormed beneath her nightclothes, caressing and squeezing: Melanie’s hopeful smile. Other mothers peering into the pram of her newborn; their faces crumbling. Emptied. Wintertime: snowflakes dancing and swirling around a streetlamp. Snarling puppies ostracising their sibling with the dragging back legs; the mother too; the bitch’s black lips curling upwards, warning, growling her disapproval. Springtime: making daisy-chains in the warming grass. Butterflies and coloured shadows; bright laughter fading.

Autumn. No more daisy-chains – Geoff's manly tears on the day of the funeral.

"I'm the one," Janice said.

Geoff's heavy breathing didn't interrupt itself.

The instant pain ripped through her. Janice cried out. It had been so long. Geoff moved slowly until he found his rhythm. Each tentative thrust tore at her. Janice lay there without moving, her lower lip clamped between her teeth to increase the voluptuous, searing torture.

"That's it," she said. This was what she deserved.

Had it not been for her faulty make-up, her weakened genes, Melanie would have been born a normal child. She, Janice, was responsible.

Geoff's fierce breathing had turned to grunts, the sound of an animal. From Melanie's room, the puppy's whimpering had graduated to howling, which, in turn, set off a howling chorus from the room below. The pitiful canine lament invaded Janice's understanding of the moment. She was on the cusp of something, of a discovery.

Geoff's primal scream coincided with, or triggered maybe, that discovery. Janice, too, released an elongated shriek as the flames slashed and burned. Internal combustion.

"Kill me," she roared. "Kill me."

No Burden He

Like demons from a child's imagination, they oozed from behind a copse of trees: six or seven of them. Hoodys. Their buzz haircuts, vacant eyes and scrunched-up features filled my bladder.

Cornered. Trapped. Any attempt to flee would justify the chase: a pair of sickly antelopes strayed from the herd; the hyena clan spurred into action – cleansers of the contaminated, purifiers of the stricken.

"Be ready," I muttered to Kerr.

One of them, with a battle-scarred face and flaring nostrils, the alpha male I guessed, reached us first. He stopped a few feet away in our path and gestured that the cackling clan hold back. A large, knobbly Adam's apple scampering up the alpha-male's neck towards his chin and dropping like a guillotine churned the Saturday morning fry-up in my stomach.

Keeping the same pace, I nodded, mumbled a "How's it going?" and tried to steer Kerr and me around him.

"What did you call me?" he asked, and snatched at my arm as I twisted by.

"Get your hand off me," I said, turning to face the inevitable. Better to do it with bravado.

"Your back, Jayo," Kerr's voice warned.

I twisted round to catch a silver sheet of light explode across my vision.

Took me seconds maybe to realise I'd been struck hard to the temple. Someone had hit me with such force I think I was out briefly. My groggy attempts to scrabble off the prickly earth brought half the pack atop me, their snarling voices driving kicks and blows that caught me in the ribs, the groin and the back of my head.

No chance to retaliate, to rage against the unprovoked

violation. Through breathlessness, the internal flames whipping through my body and the frenzy of incoherent shouts and sickening ululations, I was aware of my kid brother Kerr's screaming voice, stuttered and punctuated by balled fists slammed into his face, and by boots primed to maim. And not a thing I could do. My arms as lifeless as the day I helped our dad carry over a thousand concrete blocks from the front to the back garden the time we built the extension.

And then Kerr's voice began to fade. Into my head was poured something sludgy, a thick, dark substance that swallowed up colour and shape, clogged my ears, took away the pain, erased all sense of guilt, and replaced helplessness with indifference.

"Lads. Lads. Are you okay, lads?" a man's voice that wasn't our father's voice called from across millions of miles of ocean.

Unable to open my eyes, I felt the warm, salty wetness of the ocean's waves lapping about my face. I'd been carried to the shore. A coughing and spluttering bout removed the last of the drowning waters from my lungs.

"Ranger. Get out of that. Ranger. Come here, boy."

My eyes open now, I saw an old man holding back a black dog by the collar.

"Sorry about that," the man said. "Ranger was only saying 'Hello'. He won't bite you."

"Where's Kerr?" I slurred, turning over and getting to my knees so I could see above the tall ragwort weeds. I wiped the doggy stink from my face with my forearm.

"Your friend is here, son," the old man said. "But he seems to be out cold. What happened to yous in anyway?"

While trying to wake Kerr up, I explained to the old man as best I could. But when Kerr didn't respond, after I'd tapped him a few times on the cheek, and listened to his low breathing, I took him by the shoulders and shook him. "Kerr," I shouted. "They've gone, Kerr. We have to go home now. Kerr."

"An ambulance, son," the old man said. "He needs an ambulance."

The old man was right. But when I dipped my hand into my pockets for my phone, it was gone. And so was Kerr's. The hoodys had taken them.

The old man said he couldn't help me there, when I asked him. Wouldn't even know how to use one, he said. "Them and those bloody whatdoyoumecallit? Bloody computer yokes."

He suggested that I run into town for help, as I'd be quicker than an auld fella like him. That's how he described himself. He offered to stay and look after Kerr till I got back.

I gave it about a nanosecond's thought, and decided against the idea. What if the hoodys came back to finish what they'd started? Would he get his stupid dog to lick them to death? And, besides, there were stories about priests and stuff with kids; old priests as ancient as the 'auld fella'. On the news I'd heard it. You couldn't trust anyone.

"You're alright, mister," I said. "I'll take him myself."

"No," the old man said. "You can't move him. He might be hurted."

I ignored the old man's high-pitched warnings and protestations, and struggled to get Kerr's unconscious body across my shoulders, the way I'd seen soldiers do with fallen comrades in movies.

Since we were little kids I'd given Kerr thousands of piggybacks. But as soon as I'd hitched him into a fireman's lift, it felt like I had a castle on my back. On bended knees, I shifted him about till I found my centre of gravity. I pitched forward, but only made it as far as the canal banks, about twenty paces away, before my legs gave out and my lungs were screaming. Felt as though I was trying to suck in air through a bent straw.

I lay there on the worn track next to Kerr's unconscious body; the old man's faraway voice as incidental and futile as the birdsong dripping from the surrounding trees. Overhead, the clouds drifted and reshaped into mountains that then crumbled into winged creatures and four-legged beasts, which, in turn, stretched and contorted into faces I thought I recognised.

Seconds or minutes passed, I can't be sure, before my head cleared and the oxygen flowed freely to my lungs. My body, however, refused to move. I was exhausted. With strength enough to pull myself through the reeds, I slid my arm down the bank to the water's edge, scooped up some water and pressed my hand to my forehead. And then I did the same for Kerr, stroking his enflamed cheeks with my palm.

Perhaps it was the old man's monotonous voice banging on about my being a fit young fellow and him an old man unable to fetch help that did it. Or could be that subconsciously I knew that Kerr needed immediate attention to prevent the unacceptable outcome – or a combination of both factors – but, from somewhere, I mustered up the energy to start screaming and yelling for help.

I shouted and roared until I felt as though I'd slashed my throat from inside. And I would have gone on shouting forever, too, or until my voice surrendered, if a man on the far side of the canal bank hadn't shouted over and learned from the old man that Kerr and me needed an ambulance.

By that evening I'd been released from hospital and was lying in my top bunk trying to make sense of what had happened. For the first time in ten years, I was alone in

Kerr's and my bedroom. I woke up a few times, imagining Kerr had awoken me from the bottom bunk asking me if I was awake. Kerr always hated being awake by himself.

Like a steel-grey blanket of sky, despair descended on our house over the next few days. Kerr was in a coma. The doctors had no idea if he'd pull through, and everybody blamed me for taking him to a place I'd been warned a million times to stay away from.

I reasoned with our dad, the only one who'd listen to me, that Kerr probably just needed sleep. I reminded him of the time Dad ran over our cat with the front wheel of the car. Dad put her in a cardboard box next to the central heating in the living room. The cat slept for nearly a week, before coming back to life, as though a tonne of tin and steel hadn't pressed her into the gravel.

Our mum was hysterical most of the time. She reminded me of one of those Arab women on TV wailing and beating the air with her fists, cursing God, herself and the world. She terrified me.

The call came in the middle of the night on the fifth day. Kerr was awake. Defying all expectation, he'd come out of his coma.

The three of us – Dad, Mum and me – pulled on our clothes and sped through the night for the hospital. For once Mum didn't tell Dad to slow down.

On arrival at the hospital, a man in a white coat and with one of those things around his neck met us in the ward and spoke softly to Mum and Dad. I heard him say he was sorry. Before we approached Kerr's bed, Dad put his hand on my shoulder and told me that Kerr wasn't quite better yet, and that I wasn't to excite him in any way.

Kerr's eyes were open. And on his face a smile, a smile I quickly realised wasn't really a smile. Mum was crying again and when she tried to speak to him, these terrible sounds leaked from her. She held her palm over her mouth, and her face crumpled. Hospital staff supported her and helped her to a plastic chair.

Dad told Kerr we were all waiting for him to come home, and that as soon as he was fit and strong we were going to Disneyland in Paris. Dad drew me in front of him, got me to say something to my brother. I couldn't think of anything to say, so I told him all about the computer game I'd played before I went to bed, who I'd beaten up or killed and my final score. But you could tell that Kerr wasn't getting any of it. He was just following the direction of the voices, the way an animal follows sounds.

Kerr didn't make very much progress over the coming weeks. Without him to play with and talk to, I had plenty of time to think. It came to me one day that the Kerr in the hospital, grinning like some idiot, wasn't the Kerr who used to be my little brother. He'd lost something. What exactly it was he'd lost I couldn't say. But, whatever it was, it happened that day we were waylaid by the hoodys.

It got me thinking about my last birthday, my fourteenth, when Dad gave me a pocketknife for my birthday. One of the best presents I ever got. Besides the blade, there was a spoon, a fork, a screwdriver, a miniature saw, a scissors, a nail file and a yoke for pushing back your cuticles. Kerr and me whizzed off to the fields, where we flung the knife through the air, letting it somersault and spear into the earth. Within minutes of the game, Kerr had thrown it too far and lost it. We searched for hours but couldn't locate it.

For weeks afterwards, we scoured that field, until one day I found it. By then the weather had corroded the metal and none of the tools would open. But that didn't matter. I was overjoyed that nobody else had found the knife. The knife belonged to me. I had it once more.

More a feeling than a logical thought, I felt the same way about Kerr. The something terribly important that Kerr had lost that day we were ambushed by the hoodys lay in and around where we'd been attacked. I had to find it before a stranger stumbled upon it.

Felt like I was going crazy and my head no longer worked properly. I went on the hop from school and got myself to the woods behind the canal. With no idea what I was looking for, I searched for the elusive something that had fallen from Kerr that day when I, as his older brother, failed to protect him the way a big brother is supposed to watch over his younger brother.

I learned the ways of wild things, discovered that so long as you moved cautiously in the shadows, utilising all your senses, frequently laying low, and didn't put yourself about in bright sunshine, you could go undetected. I took supplies with me: sandwiches, chocolate and bottled water, in place of my schoolbooks. I got to know the hoodys' routine. From the hidden branches of nearby trees, I spied on them during their drinking sessions. Even though the weather was still quite warm, they lit fires and paraded round the flames like Red Indians. Irrelevant to recall the details, some of the other antics they got up to brought a cold sweat to my brow and stirred the contents of my stomach.

One Saturday afternoon in late autumn, I'd been wandering the fields before the hoodys' usual arrival time, just after 2.30 pm, when I saw the familiar figure of the lead hoody, the alpha male, climb over the broken wall from the canal. He was alone. Inside my chest there struck up a mild thumping, and my knees weakened.

Without foreplanning or consideration, I removed my leather belt from my waist. Letting the skull and crossbones buckle dangle, I wrapped the other end about my hand.

Ensuring he was definitely alone, I crouched down behind a bramble bush in the hoodys' drinking area, a base they had fashioned with corrugated iron and broken branches in a natural clearing among the trees.

I could hear my own blood pounding in my head as he kind of walked and trotted closer. I then waited until he had seated himself atop a half-squashed oil drum, uncapped his bottle and began to sing. He sang a gravelish, off-key version of an Oasis song. A song I hated.

And then the moment arrived – to fight or flee? Images in my head from that day in early summer when he and his hyena clan had taken forever Kerr's understanding of who and what he was made my decision for me.

I charged at him with such speed, he spilled over his front a lot of the crap he'd been pouring into his gullet. But he was quicker than I expected. Somehow he was on his feet and facing me, the upturned bottle raised above his head, its contents splashing down his arm and to the ground. From his twisted face he snarled a nasally snarl that raked my insides.

I swung the buckle at him. He sidestepped, causing the buckle to rap me on my own wrist. I sucked up the pain, turning it into something else. He slammed the bottle hard on the old oil drum, the hollow boom causing a pigeon to flap madly from a nearby tree. The bottle remained intact.

The next swing of my belt connected with his hand. He dropped the bottle and bellowed, holding the stricken hand. His Adam's apple rocketed up his neck and crashed back to his throat like one of those discs that hits the gong in a fairground. I hit him again, across the face this time. And again – the backs of his legs, his side, working into a rhythm, until he was curled up on the ground, threatening me with what he was going to do to me and, simultaneously, begging me to leave him alone.

"You're fucking dead, you bollix. Agghh, no, please leave us alone. Just wait until I fucking. Fuck. That hurts. I'm sorry, man, I didn't mean to. Shit, me fucking hand."

I flailed and thrashed him until tears of anger and revenge bled down my cheeks, and no more threats or cowering came from the shaven-headed prick lying unconscious in his own urine-stained jeans.

Before walking away, I fought a very real urge to pick up the hoody's wine bottle, smash it on a rock, and ram the jagged edge into his Adam's apple. Instead I bent down, grabbed him by the ears, raised his head and roared into his ear that this was his punishment for what he had done to Kerr. I then spat into his scrunched-up features, slammed his head into the fire-hardened earth, kicked him into the back and walked away.

A few weeks since I'd last visited Kerr with Mum and Dad, I went with them that afternoon. I whispered into Kerr's ear everything I'd done to the lead hoody. What could have been a tear slipped from the corner of one of his eyes, and I think his fixed smile wavered. But maybe I was imagining it.

"One down," I whispered to him as we – Mum, Dad and I – said our goodbyes. "Six to go," I promised.

For the Children

"A coward as well as a bastard." Larissa's words battled against the mocking December wind that, all in a breath, had crumpled her flimsy red umbrella and broken most of its spines. "Look at what you've done to us," she added, as though he hadn't abandoned forever her and their children and was walking next to her along the canal bank.

Before pushing on with the two youngest, the baby inside the vintage Hubcar pram and the three-year-old perched at the end facing her, Larissa dashed the broken umbrella into the swollen canal waters.

Only when the boy had emerged from behind his hands did she realise the confusion she had caused her child. The wail he could no longer suppress played through the howling wind, his cheeks fire engine-red, and his eyes filled with all the hurt that ever was.

"No, no, sweetheart," she said, stopping and taking the boy in her arms. "Mummy's not cross with you. Mummy's just tired. That's all. I'm sorry, pet. Poor baby. Poor baby Shane." So easy to forget that he too was still a baby.

Five of them – that bastard's legacy. Hadn't even the courage to take them with him. And his timing: one month before Christmas. He got out just before the banks took everything: their home, the business and their properties. His one-way ticket a bullet; something he used to joke about. Selfish bastard.

Now here she was, two days to Christmas, barely keeping them fed and clothed, living in a one-bedroom council flat with fluorescent lighting and a small gas heater, but unable to pay the gas bill.

She swivelled from the waist, pressing baby Shane so close she felt the freezing rain run off his hood and down her neck. Over the boy's shoulder the wind whipped up spray from the tops of the frantic canal waters. As always, Larissa imagined herself dressed in black beneath a cold moon, wrestling to hold the five children beneath the murky waters until they were safe. Before she too would lie face down embracing her peaceful brood, about her the sea of night closing, enveloping her, reuniting them, a family forever.

But Jesus Christ, he'd left her with five of them. Two, even three, and she might have had the strength to save them, to deliver them to a better place. But five.

The images shifted to the wide-eyed faces of the twins beneath the brackish waters, their hollow mouths bubbling, their arms and legs thrashing and flailing while she held each below the shallow waters. And then their maddened intake of breath, their coughing up the icy water when she released them in her efforts to catch Heather who had escaped from her with the baby and was screaming her way back to where Shane, half-submerged, huddled behind his hands in the reeds at the canal bank. In the backdrop, squares of light flicking to life in the windows of the nearby flat complex, their new home; silhouetted figures, late-night revellers, with undefined features appearing from nowhere on the banks of the canal, pointing and bellowing accusations; a police siren drawing near, the blinding headlights, its flashing blue light; the car grinding to a stop; doors cracking open, the uniformed driver and passenger spilling into the night, the guards' faces bloodless and illuminated, bloated with authority and disgust at something they could never understand: the ferocity of a mother's love and her ruthless endeavours to protect and save her children.

"Mummy, Mummy," Shane continued. She'd heard him but hadn't heard him.

"What is it, love?" She quickened her pace. The day

was already darkening. The older ones would be out in five minutes. She wouldn't reach the school in time.

"When is Daddy coming home?"

The invisible hand, poised in accustomed readiness, plunged down Larissa's throat, grasped her stomach and squeezed. She had yet to locate a satisfactory answer for a three-year-old mind. A question asked a thousand times.

"We're late, love. Heather and the twins will be wondering where we are." She shifted into a kind of run with the pram, but eased back to a fast walking pace. The soaked leaves were treacherous.

"When, Mummy? When is he?" The boy held a corner of his hood down and peered up at her with one eye, his features clenched against the cold.

"Oh, look at the lights on the Christmas tree."

The boy twisted round and tore off his hood for a better look.

"No, Shane. You have to keep your hood up." She pulled it back into place.

The boy caught hold of its edge to keep it from blowing off.

Coming towards her then, a rough-looking young couple holding hands. She willed herself to avoid eye contact, but, like everything else, her willpower deserted her. Around the girl's mouth and nose a network of scabs, one of her puffed up eyes, eggplant purple. As they passed her, the male clutching the female's hand challenged Larissa with fixed eyes and scrunched up features to look away.

"What the fuck you looking at?" a nasally voice, the male's, called after her from behind.

"Fucking auld bitch." The female's.

God she hated this place.

"Choo," Shane said as she pushed the pram up the

sloped bank that brought them out onto the bridge. "Mummy. Choo. A train, Mummy."

"Not now, love. Please. Mummy might slip."

Momentary panic clutched her by the throat at the school gate. The kids. She couldn't see the kids. Although Heather was old enough, she vowed always to collect them. You couldn't trust this neighbourhood.

"They're over there, missus," an overweight mother said. Two small girls, replicas of the mother in miniature scowled up at Larissa. The mother chucked her chin to the other side of the road. "Look it."

On the far pavement Heather had the twins by their hands and was stepping into the road.

"No, Heather," Larissa shouted. "Stay there. Wait for the Lollipop man."

"You're welcome in anyway," the fat mother's voice said next to her.

"What?" Larissa said, turning to the cluster of gabbing mothers and their children.

"Oh, yes. Sorry. Thank you. Excuse me."

"You're alright. Happy Christmas, missus."

"Oh, yes. Happy Christmas," Larissa said.

The wind and rain eased off on their way home to the flats.

Smelly. That's what Heather said they called her in school that day. The reason she'd crossed the road. They chanted it. And went on chanting after the bell went. Through a voice coming undone, Heather repeated it in the singsong tones of her classmates: "Smelly, smelly, smelly. Nothing in her belly."

Larissa brought her trembling fingers to her mouth, closed her eyes and bit down. This is what they'd come to. Where once she had to choose between a Mercedes and an SUV, now she had to decide between washing powder or the children going hungry.

The twins, five years younger than eleven-year-old Heather, giggling together, repeated the chant. One of them held his nose and called Heather 'pongy'.

Larissa's open hand connected with the boy's face so forcefully he slipped to the sodden pavement. "Don't you ever," she said to the boy as she dragged him to his feet. "Never ever. She's your sister."

The slapped boy, his hand rubbing his cheek, locked his eyes to the ground for a number of seconds, his face astonished, before exploding into uncontrollable bawling. This set off his twin, as it generally did. Heather was now crying too, as was the baby, and Shane was emerging from one of his silent, open-mouthed wails, the type that turned his face pink and would bring on the inevitable bout of coughing that made him look like he was choking to death.

"Sweets," Larissa said. She pushed the pram forward, avoiding the judgemental faces in the street. "Who's for sweets?" What kind of monster was she turning into?

By the time they reached the Spar, the children had mostly cried themselves out.

"Hello, love," the guy in the shop doorway greeted her.

"Yes," Larissa said. "Hello." A wave of nausea splashed about her stomach. Her head felt light.

"Nippy, isn't it?" He worked his hands together, brought them to his mouth and made a blowing sound.

"Uncle Zebb. Uncle Zebb," one of the twins said, pulling on the security man's jacket.

"What's up, buster?" He ruffled the boy's wet hair, but his attention he kept on Larissa.

"Are you coming over to our place for Christmas?" the twin asked.

"Don't know, son. That's up to your ma." He smirked and winked at her.

Larissa nodded. Mute.

He wrung his hands together again. “Nice one. I’ll have something for the chisellers so.”

“Deadly.” The twin ran into the shop to tell his twin, the one who’d been slapped.

“It’s just meself is on,” he said to Larissa. He spoke out the side of his mouth. “Go ahead, love.”

He shifted sideways to let her squeeze by, but not enough to allow her entry without brushing off his flabbiness. And she felt his meaty hand palming and squeezing her ass. The cloying smell of cooked meat and stale tobacco was worse than his touch.

Once the children had chosen their treats and dumped them on top of the pram cover, Larissa told them to go and look at the comics. Uncle Zebb would bring them comics on Christmas Eve. They had to choose which ones they wanted. Then, ensuring she wasn’t being watched, she slipped the chocolate and crisps under the pram cover with the baby.

Something beat behind Larissa’s eyes, and her legs threatened to buckle. She leaned over the pram handlebar. She’d never get used to this. Never wanted to.

The packet of Daz she concealed under the cover was too bulky; too obvious. She decided against the routine that had worked those other times: going to the counter and making a minimal purchase, a couple of toffee bars or a box of matches. Just to *take the dirty look off.* An expression that bastard used to use. She wished she could stop hearing his voice in her head.

“Excuse me, madam,” a voice called behind her, a voice crowded with superiority and self-justification.

“Quick, children,” she shouted to where they were clambering around the newsstand. “Quick. Quick.”

“Madam. Excuse me. Wait.”

Outside the shop, the security man was hunched down

in a kind of seating position, his arms crossed and dangling over one knee. With him was Heather, half-seated on his other leg. The two were smiling and whispering, but nearly toppled over on seeing Larissa trundling from the shop; as though they'd been rumbled engaged in something so sordid, she didn't even want to consider what. A conclusion Larissa wouldn't reach till later. Because right then she was too caught up in getting away before the shop manager, or whoever he was, put his hand on her shoulder.

"Run, Heather. Come on. Let's go."

Heather obeyed Larissa and ran with her and the other children, but was quick to tell her, in an out-of-breath, shaky voice, that she hated her, and that she always made a show of her, and that as soon as she was sixteen, she was gone.

"I'm gone," she said. "I am so fucking out of here."

"Don't you dare," Larissa said. Her heart was banging so hard inside her chest from the exertion of their escape she thought she might collapse. Panting and clutching her throat, she turned round to look back at the shop. She thought she could make out in the distance somebody talking to the security man in the pool of light at the door. She wasn't sure. But none of the people in the street looked like they were chasing her and the kids.

When she managed to get some oxygen back into her lungs, she counted to ten. Another thing *he* had taught her to do.

"Look," she said to Heather. "I know it's tough right now, sweetheart. But we'll get through this. We'll make it. Okay?"

Heather ducked under Larissa's arms attached to the pram, the way she did when she was little, wrapped her arms about her and pressed her face against her chest.

"We'll make it," Larissa repeated.

“What are we going to make, Mummy,” Shane asked. “Mummy, what are we?” He waved his arms up and down like he was trying to fly.

“A family, love,” she said to the boy. “We’re going to make a proper family again.”

“With Uncle Zebb, Mummy?” one of the twins’ asked.

“Is Uncle Zebb going to be our new Daddy?” the other twin asked.

Larissa explained that Uncle Zebb was Mummy’s friend. He wasn’t really their uncle. The same way the Santa in the shopping centre wasn’t the real Santa. And nobody would ever take the place of the real Santa. Now, would they?

That got them all talking about Christmas, and what they wanted from Santa. Heather distracted them by starting up singing a Christmas carol. The younger ones joined in. They sang all the way home.

On Christmas Eve, while the younger children waited in anticipation for Santa and what he would bring, Larissa awaited, with equal anticipation, a different visitor.

He arrived just after seven.

“Mummy, it’s Uncle Zebb,” one of the twins called from the door, as if they still lived in a seven room home and he wasn’t so close she could smell him, a cocktail of alcohol, garlic and cologne.

“Yes,” she said. “Come in. Come in.”

He came at her with a small, white object in his outstretched arm. “You dropped this the other day. In the shop, like. Your man, the bloke was running after you gave it to me.”

Larissa took it. The baby’s rattle. She twisted it about in her hands and frowned at it as though she’d never in her life seen a baby’s rattle.

“Right,” she said. “Thank you. But didn’t you say…”

She glanced at the children's expectant faces and returned her attention to his empty hands.

"Of course. Certainly." He smiled a disturbing smile. "I have some parcels outside the door. A surprise like." He turned to Heather. "Do you want to give us a hand, love?"

"No," Larissa said. "I'll help you."

"Right you be," he said. "Sound."

Outside the flat door on the communal balcony were two large, green, canvas sacks, the kind Larissa's gardener used to use when working in their three-tiered garden.

"Goodness," Larissa said. "I'll have to drag this one in. What have you got in here? Bricks?"

He laughed a wheezy laugh. "Sure, leave it there, love. I got them this far. I'll manage the both of them. One at a time through the door." He laughed another needless laugh.

Handing out selection boxes, the comics and fizzy drinks for the kids, Zebb explained that the presents that were wrapped weren't to be opened till the morning.

"Flats is different," he said. "You see, there isn't no chimneys in flats, so Santa can't get in like. That's where I come in." He laughed again. "I got onto the man in red, what?"

Larissa watched from Zebb to the twins' and Shane's puzzled faces, frowning at him.

"The man in red," he repeated. "The big man. The fat fella, Santa."

The twins exploded into laughter. Shane copied them.

"Ho, ho," Zebb said. "Anyways, I got Santa to come to my gaff early with your presents. But Santa says to me, mind, that you lot can't open them till Christmas morning. Do we have a deal?" He turned his head sideways, widened his eyes and made a face that reminded Larissa of an ape sucking in its lips.

When the kids had eaten their fill, Larissa put them off

to bed. The sooner they were asleep, she told them, the sooner the morning.

Sitting beside Zebb on the couch that doubled as her bed, she told him how impressed she was with his way with the children.

"I've got rakes of nephews and nieces," he said. "They cost me a fortune." No laugh this time. His narrow eyes slid around her body.

Larissa sucked in the wall of her gum, clamping it between her canines and worried the flesh till she got the metallic, coppery taste. *For the children*, she took up the usual mantra in her head. *For the children. For their sake*.

While he used the bathroom, she tried to imagine what he'd be like were he to shed a few stone, get some dental work and maybe dress up in a suit occasionally. She gave up. The task was too great.

From the bathroom, the sound of the toilet flushing and then the tap being turned. A hawking sound followed by a spit.

"When you're ready," he said, stepping into the room.

"Wait," she said. She got up from the couch and pushed it in front of the children's bedroom door. Zebb helped her.

Shivering, she lay down on the couch, one arm across her breasts the other below her stomach. The cold had seeped right into her bones.

She waited while he pulled off his T-shirt and worked his great legs free of his dark combats. On his face as he approached her a look of hunger, of hatred, like the face of the young man who'd cursed her on the canal bank. Contorted features at complete odds with the face he wore earlier with the children.

For the children. For the children. For the children.

His huge body mantling hers was like the slow descent of Death. Larissa closed her eyes. Through her nostrils came the stink of decay and corruption, the stench that pervades the senses when you lie down in murky waters and accept the dark veil as an escape from the intensity of too much light.

Atop her he wheezed and grunted his way into a steady rhythm, his icy fingers probing, testing, squeezing, the only one to understand the ferocity of a mother's love and her ruthless endeavours to protect and save her children.

About the Author

Steve Wade's award-winning short fiction has been widely published in literary magazines and anthologies. His work has been broadcast on national and regional radio. He has had stories short-listed for the Francis McManus Short Story Competition and for the Hennessy Award. His stories have appeared in over fifty print publications, including Crannog, New Fables, and Aesthetica Creative Works Annual. His unpublished novel, *On Hikers' Hill* was awarded First Prize in the abook2read.com competition, with Sir Tim Rice as the top judge. He has won First Prize in the Delvin Garradrimna Short Story Competition on a number of occasions. Winner of the Short Story category in the Write by the Sea writing competition 2019. His short stories have been nominated for the PEN/O'Henry Award, and for the Pushcart Prize.

Other Writing by Steve Wade

Till the Embers Turn to Ashes

in

New Fables, Summer 2010

Published by Sofawolf Press

Travel to strange and wonderful places with more of the best writing from furry fandom and beyond. Meet a dog-soldier struggling to grow up in a normal family and a team of battle-weary horses put out to pasture. A half-wolf laments the loss of her pack as she is forced to run the Minotaur's maze to escape slavery, and a faithful friend looks back on his best friend's life. The moon inspires in a lovely poem, and reveals a mysterious coyote in old California.

These diverse stories continue the age-old tradition of telling human stories with animal themes. Alienation, betrayal, loyalty, and love shine in the writing of the New Fables authors, not only through the stories, but through their mastery of expression and form.

Order from Sofawolf Press:

https://sofawolf.com/products/new-fables-2010?sku=NF10

The Dog of War
in

Plight of the Rhino

Published by Springbok Publications

The stories and poems, written by international writers, depict wildlife in all its glory. The book will take you on a journey across continents and introduce you to some iconic as well as lesser known wildlife species. These heartfelt stories recognise the joys of the animal kingdom and the heartache of poaching.

A minimum of £1 from the sale of each book will be donated to **Save the Rhino International**. To find out more about its rhino conservation work please visit www.savetherhino.org.

Order from Amazon:

Paperback: ISBN 978-1-493659-60-9
eBook: ASIN B00H2XDHD0

Other Publications by Bridge House

Days Pass like a Shadow

by Paula R.C. Readman

Within the pages of *Days Pass like a Shadow* are thirteen dark tales covering the theme of death and loss. At the centre of every story is a beating heart. For the reader to make the journey to that centre, along the flowing veins of the words, all they need is a few minutes during a lunch break, or at the end of the day. The reader will be introduced to a rich and diverse collection of characters - a gardener, a serial killer, a time traveller, a sleepwalker and many more.

Thirteen very different stories, each in its own time and location, but all connected by death and loss. There is something here for everyone. I enjoyed each and every story. You are pulled in from the very first word." (*Amazon*)

Order from Amazon:

Paperback: ISBN 978-1-907335-80-8
eBook: ISBN 978-1-907335-81-5

Last Chance Salon

by FJ McNeill

"Who was I kidding? I wasn't a successful businessman running an empire from a luxury penthouse. I was a chain-smoking, fifty-something, sometime actor in a cardigan, washed-up in a stagnant corner of south London."

When Rafe Bunce takes over a run-down hair salon in Penge, he hopes to make a success of his life at last. Not content with improving his own fortunes, he is soon meddling in his customers' lives, too – with bittersweet results.

The stories in *Last Chance Salon* touch on the hopes and dreams, big and small, which we all carry inside us.

Tales from Where the Wall is Cracked

by Paul Bradley

In this debut collection of short stories Paul Bradley takes a look at how extra-ordinary everyday life can be. Kitchen sink realism, magic realism and humour are deployed to present a variety of characters, many of whom live on the margins and cannot or will not fit in. In these pages you will meet a walrus man, a mynah bird called Hitler, Kendo Nagasaki, gypsy Romana, a lonely signaller and many others in an eclectic variety of edgy tales from where the wall is cracked. Wherever possible, light shines through.

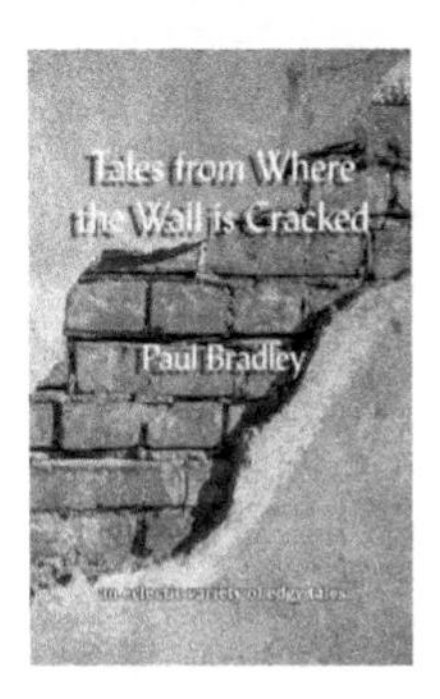

"Thoroughly enjoyable from beginning to end with each story bringing the seemingly ordinary to very colourful life. Original, quirky, funny, thought provoking… and more. Definitely recommend!" (*Amazon*)

Order from Amazon:

Paperback: ISBN 978-1-907335-74-7
eBook: ISBN 978-1-907335-75-4

Lightning Source UK Ltd.
Milton Keynes UK
UKHW021854111020
371403UK00005B/49